A Wizard and a Warlord

BOOKS BY CHRISTOPHER STASHEFF

The Warlock
The Warlock in Spite of Himself
King Kobold Revived
The Warlock Unlocked
Escape Velocity
The Warlock Enraged
The Warlock Wandering
The Warlock Is Missing
The Warlock Heretical
The Warlock's Companion
The Warlock Insane
The Warlock Rock
Warlock and Son

The Rogue Wizard
A Wizard in Mind
A Wizard in Bedlam
A Wizard in War
A Wizard in Peace
A Wizard in Chaos
A Wizard in Midgard
A Wizard and a Warlord

The Warlock's Heirs
A Wizard in Absentia
M'Lady Witch
Quicksilver's Knight
The Spell-Bound Scholar

Starship Troupers
A Company of Stars
We Open on Venus
A Slight Detour

The Rhyming Wizard
Her Majesty's Wizard
The Oathbound Wizard
The Witch Doctor
The Secular Wizard
My Son the Wizard

The StarStone
The Shaman
The Sage

Christopher Stasheff

A Wizard and a Warlord

A Tom Doherty Associates Book
New York

This is a work of fiction. All the characters and events portrayed in this novel are either fictitious or are used fictitiously.

A WIZARD AND A WARLORD

This book is printed on acid-free paper.

A Tor Book
Published by Tom Doherty Associates, LLC
175 Fifth Avenue
New York, NY 10010

www.tor.com

Library of Congress Cataloging-in-Publication Data

Stasheff, Christopher.
A wizard and a warlord / Christopher Stasheff.—1st ed.
p. cm.—(The rogue wizard)
"A Tom Doherty Associates book."
ISBN 0-312-86649-6 (acid-free paper)
1. Wizards—Fiction. 2. Warlords—Fiction. I. Title.

PS3569.T3363 W585 2000
813'.54—dc21

99-057830

First Edition: February 2000

Printed in the United States of America

0 9 8 7 6 5 4 3 2 1

A Wizard and a Warlord

1

The transparent wall curved up to form a ceiling filled with the glory of a million stars; below glowed the bank of screens that showed the views around the ship. A smaller screen, set into the surface of the console in the center of the room, lit the craggy features of the giant who sat poring over a database. He was Magnus d'Armand, itinerant revolutionary, and the starlit room was the bridge of his spaceship Herkimer.

"So there you are!"

Magnus braced himself even as he looked up; Alea was out for blood again. "Of course."

She stood in the hatchway, fairly glowing with anger—tall, almost as tall as he, with a face that some would have called angular but that he thought lovely. Even in the loose light blue shipboard fatigues, her slender figure made his breath catch.

She strode into the room, fairly sizzling with outrage. "What are you doing in here? You're always in the lounge!"

"The press of work, I'm afraid." Magnus gestured at the

screenful of data before him. "It's time to start thinking about the planet we've picked for a landing."

"The one *you* picked! All I did was nod and agree—not that you would have paid attention if I hadn't!"

Magnus stared, hurt. "I would have chosen another destination!"

Alea plowed right past the remark. "We're almost there. A little late to be thinking about whether or not they need us, isn't it?"

Magnus bridled at her tone but fought to hide it. The adrenaline of battle sang through his veins, and he hoped it didn't show in his eyes. "Yes, I've been remiss. I'm afraid I've been enjoying your company too much to bother doing my homework."

"Enjoying my company!" Alea's lip curled in scorn. "You know I'm a shrew and a termagant—and I know it, too!"

"We do have some spirited discussions," Magnus admitted, "but they're enjoyable in their way." He frowned. "Have you changed your mind, then? Is the visit not worth our time?"

"Are there enough people to warrant it?" Alea countered. "Three huge continents, but only the fourth one, the one that's almost small enough to call an island, has been colonized."

"I don't think the worth of a people depends upon their number," Magnus said gravely.

"But they're not exactly oppressed, are they?" Alea demanded. "Not from those pictures you showed me! No one looks to be starving, no one's wearing rags—and if there are oppressors, where do they live? We didn't see any castles, any palaces—just village after village of thatch-roofed cottages!"

"The pictures we saw when we started this trip were hundreds of years old," Magnus reminded her. "A great deal may have changed. Those castles could be there now, and the people groaning in toil."

"The orbital survey doesn't show any castles on hilltops,"

Alea snapped, "and you did it yesterday. It shows only temples—and there aren't even any cities around them."

"Well, some of the towns are rather large," Magnus said, "and there's one of them for every province, with villages around it."

"You're seeing provinces where they don't exist! It takes more than a river or a mountain chain to make a political division."

"Still, I'd prefer to think of them as Neolithic city-states."

"When your 'cities' are scarcely more than large towns?" Alea said scornfully.

"Athens wasn't much more, by modern standards," Magnus said judiciously, "and it governed the farms and villages all around it."

"Just because most of the land is cultivated doesn't mean the towns govern the countryside. You might as well say the temples on top of those round hills rule the farmers! After all, they build their houses round as the hills, don't they?"

Magnus stared at her. "What a remarkable insight! Here I'd put it down to standard Neolithic architecture, but you're right! They're building the houses in imitation of the holy hills!"

Alea made an impatient, dismissive gesture; she wasn't fishing for compliments at the moment. "That's beside the point. What matters is that whatever form of government those people has, it works for them! They're well fed and well housed. Why wouldn't they be happy?"

"Because they might not be free," Magnus said. "If a girl has to marry whomever the priests tell her and a boy can never leave the county in which he was born, can they ever be content?"

"Yes, if the girl happens to love that man and the boy is happy where he is!" Alea shot back. "Sometimes the priests do have insight, you know."

"Sometimes," Magnus agreed. "I can see you might think they're too well-off to be worth a visit, but something bothers me about the setup. It's probably right, but possibly wrong, very wrong. There have been civilizations before this that nourished their people's bodies well but left their souls starving. These people may be prosperous but miserable."

"Probably! May be! We're traveling a hundred light-years for something that's *possibly* wrong! What if we get there and learn that everything's fine?"

"I'll rejoice," Magnus said. "But we might land and find the people in rags with aristocrats lording it over them. Either way, *someone* should care enough to find out what has happened to these people over the centuries."

"Why? What could we do about it? Even if we bring back word, who would care?"

"True, all the descendants of their relatives will have died long ago." Magnus sighed. "And only historians would be interested. But I can't help worrying that we may find them exploited unmercifully, as in so many other lost colonies. I'll always regret not going there if I don't find out."

"If! *If!*" Alea threw up her hands in exasperation. "Are we to spend the rest of our lives jaunting about the galaxy chasing an 'if'?"

"I know it seems a waste of our time and effort," Magnus said ruefully, "but anything could have happened to them." He forced a smile. "They might even have developed a shining Utopia with the answers to the questions that torture all souls."

"It's the hunger that tortures the bellies and the brutality of the masters we should be worrying about—and we've no reason to think these people have either!"

"That's true," Magnus agreed, "but we might find them living just as their ancestors did. What if oppression has kept them from advancing?"

"What if advances are really steps backward?" Alea snapped.

"From all those books Herkimer has showed me, it seems every time your race made another leap in progress, it cost them dearly by raising two problems for every one it solved."

It had become *his* race now, Magnus noted, though as far as he knew, she was human, too. "Yes—what good does it do to save a mother and child at birth if they die from starvation two years later? Still, if they've multiplied to the point of overpopulation, we can at least show them some modern farming techniques and boost their food production."

"If!" Alea stormed. "I can't waste my life waiting to find out if any of your 'ifs' are worth it!" She spun on her toe and stalked out.

Magnus slumped in his seat with a sigh. He had known she was spirited—that was one of the qualities that had prompted him to invite her to leave her medieval planet and join him in traveling from star to star trying to free the oppressed peoples of the colony planets—but he hadn't expected her to be so turbulent. "You don't suppose she really wants to turn back, do you, Herkimer?"

"No, Magnus," said the tranquil voice of the ship's computer. "I think she has been confined too long in a limited space with only you for company."

"And I'm scarcely the most congenial of companions," Magnus said with a sardonic smile.

"I would not have said that," the computer demurred, "and she does have her own suite with electronic 'windows' that will show her a very convincing illusion of the landscape of her home—but it is only an illusion."

"So cabin fever strikes," Magnus said with a sigh.

"She only has to come out into the rest of the ship if she wants to, Magnus," the computer reminded.

"Which she does every day," Magnus said, "and I suppose I should feel complimented, though it's hard to believe you're likable when the only other person you see rants and raves at you every time you see her."

"That has only begun this last month," Herkimer reminded, "and we have been under way for three."

"True, true—and even though she's had the distractions of all your learning programs, she must still find it hard to bear. I know I did on my first few trips."

"Very true. Still, I think you should feel complimented that she feels safe in venting her anger on you."

"Oh, I'm flattered past enduring," Magnus said sourly. "If she needs to do it, though, I can at least be a good enough friend to let her."

"It could be that she wishes you to be more than a friend."

Magnus felt a thrill of alarm but hid it by saying, "I doubt that highly. I think you guessed rightly when you said there might be some sort of emotional trauma in her past."

"Actually, that was your guess, Magnus, along with the speculation that the hurt may have been linked to sexual activity in some way."

"A jilting and a broken heart is most likely," Magnus mused. "She has told us about the pain of her neighbors' betrayal when her parents died, but I think the real agony of the spirit comes from some event she hasn't revealed."

"You do very well not to pry," the computer said a trifle primly. "Take it as a compliment, Magnus—that she trusts you enough to let her anger show."

"And confuses me with the man who hurt her?"

"In some way and at some level—possibly."

Alea stalked into her sitting room, wishing there had been a door to slam instead of a panel that hissed shut behind her. She threw herself down on the sofa, arms folded, ankles crossed, and seethed in silence. What was wrong with the man? Wasn't she important to him? Certainly he wasn't in love with her. Anger spurred again, all the stronger to hide the tinge of panic the thought evoked. If Magnus wasn't in love with her, why had he invited her to leave her home planet and travel with him?

Because you had nowhere else to go, came the answer, and with it, her own brand of self-honesty kicked in. There had been no future for her on Midgard, she had to admit. Then, too, Magnus had never even hinted that he saw her as anything but a friend—and who could, when she was so tall and ungainly and plain? Resentment surged again—what right did he have to tear her away from her homeland if he saw her as nothing more than a traveling companion?

Still, he had only extended the invitation; it was she who had leaped to accept it. She had been excited at the prospect of seeing new worlds—and still was. The thought of the planet they were approaching stirred that excitement again. True enough, it didn't seem all that different from her home planet of Midgard, not in the pictures, except that everyone on this new world of Brigante seemed to be more or less the same size, and their villages were smaller—with no sign of slavery, nor of battles.

It sounded rather dull, in fact, but after the constant dangers of her homeland, she could do with a little tranquility. Of course, she'd had plenty of that on the spaceship in the last three months, but to have it under an open sky and with a variety of new people—that would be thrilling! Not that she had any fault to find with Magnus, of course, except that he was always so quiet and so serious! Anger stirred again, but with it came a mental picture of him, tall and broad, a baulk of muscle taller even than herself, with the sharp-eyed look of an eagle—though with eyes that could turn gentle with concern and tenderness in an instant, brown eyes, larger than those of most men, in a face with a broad, high forehead, prominent cheekbones, straight nose, and surprisingly full lips. It seemed a sensual face, one made for passion.

Something within her churned at the thought. Angrily, she banished it for the nonsense it was; if Magnus had been made for passion, why was he so distant and withdrawn so often? Certainly he didn't find her attractive, probably didn't even see her as a woman—and she felt obscurely relieved at the thought. He would do for a traveling companion, and a very good one, but would she really want him to be anything more?

Yes, cried something within her, but another element bridled at the thought. She banished them both—Magnus was only a friend and shield-mate to her, as she was to him. He would take her to strange, exotic places and do his best to keep her safe there, as she would do to him. *Bare is the back without brother behind it,* she thought, and at last she had a brother—and if he had only a sister-at-arms, well, she would see to it that she was a better shield than any man could have been!

Not that there looked to be any need of shields or swords on Brigante; she had never seen a more peaceable-looking people in her life. She didn't really mind Magnus's choice in worlds to visit—anything strange and new was bound to be fascinating. But she did mind the fact that he had done the choosing, even though he had asked her opinion. Still, she had to admit that she hadn't objected; the world might not have been in trouble, but it had sounded interesting.

But she would have liked to have seen some sign of passion in him! Rail as she might, she only evoked that compassionate, gentle gaze of his, almost frightening in its intensity. For a moment, she imagined that intensity in an ardent lover's gaze, his sensual face burning with desire—and shuddered. No, she did not want that, not again, neither from him nor from any other man. The joy and the ecstasy were not worth the pain of being cast aside.

Still, he could show *some* sign of emotion.

"You don't think she really wants to change destinations, then?"

"Not when we have come so far, Magnus. If nothing else, I am certain she would like a few days to revel in the great outdoors with no walls about her and only the sky for ceiling."

"There is that," Magnus admitted. "I could do with a little shore leave myself. No offense, Herkimer—your accommodations are luxurious and very comforting, but I think she may have had her fill of easy living for the time being."

"Certainly a passenger aboard this ship lives better than the most wealthy landowner on Midgard," Herkimer said, "though without as much space."

"Still, it's more room than in her parents' house." Magnus frowned, still puzzling over the riddle that was Alea. "I really can't think of any way in which I might have offended her—other than in being me, that is . . ."

"You might also remember," Herkimer said judiciously, "that though you may not be the cause of her anger, you are the only target available at the moment."

Magnus digested that idea for a few minutes, then nodded slowly. "Yes, shore leave might be a good idea."

"Assuredly she should find better ways of expressing her anger," Herkimer said, "and probably will, given time."

"Meanwhile, though, I'm going to have to grin and bear it, eh?"

"You must persevere in the patience you have just demonstrated, yes." Herkimer was silent for a few minutes, then added,

2

Alea came to join him at the air lock saying, "You could have told me yourself, you know."

Magnus looked up at her in surprize. "I didn't think you wanted to hear my voice if you didn't have to."

"Oh, don't be silly," Alea scoffed. "Of course I want to talk with you." Her eyes were bright; she fairly glowed with eagerness. "What do you think they'll be like? Tall? Short? Anything like us?"

Magnus smiled, relieved at her change of mood. "I think they'll have two arms, two legs, and one head each."

She gave him a glare but was too excited to do it well. "They can't be as tall as we are, can they?"

"Well, they can, of course," Magnus said, "but they may also be much shorter. We don't have any way of judging size there—not by the height of their houses. They'll have built them to their own scale. We can be fairly sure, though, that they'll speak some variation of Terran Standard speech."

"Do all the colonies speak that way?"

"Most, though there are a few that deliberately revived an older language. The general rule is: the closer the dialect is to Terran Standard, the more rigid its government."

Alea frowned. "Then my peo—the Midgarders must have spoken an almost pure form."

"It had drifted a bit—they had worked in quite a few words from old German—but it was very easy to understand. It was interesting that the dwarves and giants had thicker accents than the Midgarders, though."

"Well, yes." Alea kept the frown, thinking. "Their governments weren't anywhere nearly as strict, after all."

Magnus replied, "By that rule, I suppose these people should have developed a dialect that's halfway to being a new language." Neolithic societies didn't usually have central governments, after all."

"I thought the Sumerians and the Egyptians were Neolithic."

"They were, but they don't seem to be the models these colonists used," Magnus said with a smile tight with irony. "They seem to have been more inclined to the practices of Native American and prehistoric Northern European cultures."

"Didn't like cities, I suppose," Alea said, "but I can't blame them—those pictures you showed me of a *real* city were enough to make me shudder."

"They have their disadvantages," Magnus admitted. "Great fun if you're rich, I understand, but I wouldn't know personally."

Alea stared at him, "You have a ship like this and you don't think you're rich?"

"It's my only asset," Magnus explained. "I'm what they call 'cash poor.' "

Herkimer's voice intruded. "Atmospheric testing complete. The oxygen-nitrogen mixture is quite breathable, though a little thinner than my shipboard atmosphere, and has no organisms that are likely to resist your broadband inoculations."

"Then we can go out?" Alea asked, eagerness barely restrained.

"You can." The air lock door slid open. "Enjoy your stay."

She waited impatiently for the local air to replace the ship's—in spite of his assurances, Herkimer didn't want to risk contamination of their only possible refuge. Magnus looked down at her fondly, remembering his own early excitement at visiting strange worlds.

"Should I call you 'Gar' again, now that we'll be ashore?" Alea asked.

"That would be wise," Gar agreed. "There's only a slight risk that there might be agents from an advanced society among these people, but I'd rather not take the chance that anyone here has heard of Magnus d'Armand."

Alea thought he was being silly—since he had been Gar Pike on six separate planets now and started some sort of revolution on each of them, the chances seemed greater that rival agents would have heard of Gar than of Magnus. Still, it was his choice. "There shouldn't be any problem with my using my own name, should there?"

"No," Magnus agreed. "I don't think anyone is tying the name Alea Larsdatter to rebellion and turbulence yet."

Alea was about to ask about that "yet" when the door slid open before her. With a shout of joy, she ran down the ramp into the fragrant spring night and the calf-high grass, swinging her traveler's staff end over end and whirling about in an impromptu dance of joy at being outside again.

Gar followed more slowly, smiling with pleasure at her delight.

Alea spun to a halt, hands on her hips, eyes flashing, teeth bared in a grin. "What monster shall we hunt, Gar Pike?"

"Why, whatever we find." Gar returned her grin. "A dictator or tyrant will do, though I'd rather have a corrupt king. Let us walk the night road and listen with our minds to the people in that little village half a mile away. Perhaps their dreams will tell us what sort of government rules this world."

"I could use the practice." Alea pivoted to stand by his side, chin high, smile tight with amusement. "After all, you've only just taught me how to read minds."

"You've only just learned," Gar corrected. "It's not the sort of thing one can teach—either you have the talent, or you don't."

"Still, it was good of you to let me practice on you. I wonder if I'll be able to read anyone else's mind yet."

"Oh, I think so." Gar felt the familiar half sickness, half elation at the thought that she might be so bonded to him as to be able to read only his own mind. He pushed the thought down into the depths from which it had come—he wanted a companion, not a lover.

He straightened, eyes losing focus as his mind opened to others' thoughts. "Let's listen here. See if you can pick up any thoughts from the village."

Alea straightened and stilled, too, letting her thoughts drift, stray, die down, and yield to those of the others on this planet. "Dreams," she said after a while, "a jumble of images that make no sense. . . . Well, no, that one makes sense, though I doubt any living woman was ever built like that . . . and a woman who misses her husband badly, though I doubt he was ever so handsome; what happened to him, I wonder?"

"Is there an overtone of grief to the thought?" Gar asked.

"Not really, only longing."

"Can you work into her dreams a wondering as to where he is?"

Alea stared up at him. "Is that right to do?"

"Not really," Gar said, "though there's no harm in listening to the thoughts people let slip, if they're not too personal."

"I skipped past those three—though this one is a bit more personal, in its way."

"Then let it pass, too," Gar said, "but work into someone else's dream a picture of a wanderer coming into the town."

Alea frowned. "That still seems like meddling."

"It is, but no more so than guiding a conversation toward information you want revealed."

"I suppose that's true," Alea allowed, and formed a mental picture of Gar walking into the village, his staff rising and falling. She was careful to imagine him a bit shorter than he was.

The dreamer's reaction startled her—a surge of delight, of anticipation, wondering what goods the peddler carried in his pack. Needles, perhaps, and sugar from the north, a few spices, seeds for strange varieties of maize and soybeans, pictures of exotic farm tools for the smith to make, and news, word of what passed in the rest of the world, perhaps even a new fable. . . .

"He certainly isn't afraid of a wanderer, this dreamer," Alea said. "It doesn't occur to him that a traveler could be anything but a peddler."

"Not even a minstrel? Sounds like a dull land," Gar said. "Let me try it on another dreamer." He frowned a moment, then said, "Another . . . another . . ." He turned back to Alea. "It's even as you say. Apparently peddlers are the only wanderers they know of."

"Let me try another possibility." Alea chose a teenage girl and worked a quartet of young men and women into her dream, entering the village with laughter and cries of greeting . . . "Well! I made the wanderers young and the whole village turned out in welcome. Apparently young folk are expected to wander and see a bit of the world."

"How do the younger locals react to them?"

"With flirtation," Alea said immediately. "I wonder how many of those young wanderers return home, and how many settle down in a village they discover in their travels."

"A good way of mixing the gene pool and avoiding inbreeding." Gar nodded approval. "Still, I would assume you and I are a little old for a *Wanderjahr.*"

"Speak for yourself; mine has just begun," Alea said. "But I do think the villagers would see us that way, so peddlers we'll be." She plucked up her nerve and demanded, "Husband and wife?"

"Or brother and sister, if anyone asks," Gar said. "For all we know, they may not see anything unusual in a man and a woman choosing to travel together. Was your band of young wanderers all of one gender?"

"No, I was careful to make them evenly split."

"We'll let experience teach us, then." Gar turned back to the spaceship. "Let's go collect a couple of packs of trade goods."

Packs they already had, for they had used them on Midgard. Alea told Herkimer what sort of trade goods her dreamer had wanted and the computer fabricated them in minutes, then added a few that had proved popular down the centuries—ribbons and beads, knives and pots, small bars of copper and tin.

"Do you play a musical instrument?" Gar asked.

"Why?" Alea looked up at him with a frown that cleared quickly. "Oh! The villagers' hunger for news and stories. I suppose peddlers here would have to be minstrels, too, wouldn't they?"

"It would probably give us an edge," Gar agreed.

"I can manage a flute." For a moment, Alea's eyes filled with tears at the memory of the lovely pipe with its inlaid flowers that the magistrate had taken from her when her mother and father had died. He had given it, along with herself, to the neighbors who had hated her parents. She thrust the thought to the back of her mind with impatience; there was no time to muse about such things now.

Equipped with everything they could think of, Gar and Alea went forth to conquer the retail trade.

Gar turned back at the foot of the ramp and said, "Up and away, Herkimer."

The ramp slid back into the ship and the air lock hatch hissed shut as the computer's external loudspeaker asked, "Shall I stay in geostationary orbit, Magnus?"

"Please do," Gar said. "We have our communicators if we need them, but we may need you to relay." He didn't say that they might also need to have the ship drop down and save them from a real predicament—it was an outside possibility, and there was no need to alarm Alea unduly.

The great golden disk rose silently into the night, drifting upward, then suddenly shooting away into the clouds. Gar and Alea watched it go. When it had disappeared, Alea turned away, giving herself a shake and saying, "Three months ago, I never would have believed such a sight."

"Six months ago," Gar countered, "I never would have believed in actual living giants. Shall we see if the local folk believe in mixed peddlers?"

They had to wait a few hours for sunrise, of course. Gar brewed coffee, assuming it would be their last taste for some time, but Alea was too excited for more than a few sips. When false dawn came she looked up, listening, then nodded in satisfaction. "They're up and about."

Gar nodded; they had both been reared in medieval societies, so it never occurred to either of them that there was anything unusual with people waking at first light. Gar had spent some time in modern cities and knew many people slept later, but to him, they seemed the odd ones. He stood up and walked to the brow of the hill and saw it was part of a long rise in the land. "We can see the village from here."

Alea came to stand beside him and nodded. "Herkimer chose our landing site well."

Gar noticed she didn't mention who had given Herkimer the criteria for the site. To give Alea her due, she probably didn't notice, either.

They watched the people moving about their cottages for a while—going out to milk the cow, slop the hogs, feed the chickens, and gather eggs. After a while, Alea said, "There doesn't seem to be any pattern to who does which task."

"Pattern?" Then Gar understood what she meant. "No. Some of the milkers are men, some are women. I wonder who's doing the cooking."

They were both quiet for a few minutes; then Alea guessed, "The old folk?"

"Seems possible," Gar allowed. "Come to think of it, I wonder how many teenagers are doing those morning chores."

"Where I came from, you started grown-up work at twelve," Alea said. "Not all of it, mind you—only men had the muscle to guide those heavy plows—but any teenage boy could chop wood."

"Here, it seems that the girls do it, too." Gar nodded toward one long-skirted figure who was wielding an ax.

"There's one who wishes she had done her chores before dinner!" Alea said. "Well, let's see what kind of welcome they'll give travelers."

The welcome was rude and abrupt, though it might have been a bit better if they had reached the village.

They managed to find a road by the simple expedient of going downhill and following the sound of water; the trackway ran beside the river, as farmers' roads often did. They had been following it for only ten minutes when Gar stiffened.

"What's the matter?" Alea asked in alarm.

"Company coming," Gar said, clipping off the words. "Armed and looking for trouble. Hide, quickly!"

Alea turned toward the brush at the roadside, then realized he was standing still and turned back. "Didn't you hear yourself? Come on!"

"Someone has to talk to them," Gar said, "or we'll never learn anything."

"Then I will." Alea came back.

"Believe me, companion, you have more to fear from them than I do," Gar said grimly, "and I shall be stronger for an ally in reserve when they think I'm alone. Hide, I beg you, or I shall have to flee with you, and we'll lose this chance for information."

"All right, be a fool if you must!" Alea said, exasperated, and turned to slip in among the underbrush. Still, he had a point—if they tried to harm him, she could leap out and strike from behind. Her heart quailed at the thought, but anyone who had fought wild dogs could summon the courage to fight wild men. Not that it would do her much good, probably, but it might give him a chance.

There they came, six men riding, with crude wooden shields slung from their saddlebows and spears in their hands. Alea shuddered at the sight of them; they were rough-looking men, all dressed alike in brown leather jerkins and trousers, several days overdue for a shave, and all glowering. They saw their quarry and yelped like hounds on a scent, kicking their horses into gallops.

Gar stood, leaning on his staff and watching, apparently tranquil and interested—but Alea knew that he was really putting no weight on the wood, that the pose was only an apparently harmless way of having both hands on a weapon.

The riders drew rein with savage cries, surrounding him and grinning. It was hard to gauge their height when they were mounted, but Alea could tell they were much shorter than Gar.

"Well, here's a big enough catch!" said one. "You're meat for the general now, fellow!"

"For the general what?" Gar asked, interested.

The riders guffawed, and the spokesman said, "General Malachi, that's what! What d' ye have in that pack there?"

"Only the usual goods," Gar said, "ribbons and needles and the like."

"Girls' stuffs," one of the men sneered, but the leader said, "Off with it, then, and hand it over!"

Gar shrugged out of the straps, changing his staff from one hand to another to do so, then dropped it at his feet. He frowned at it for a few seconds as though thinking it over, then looked up and said, "I don't think so."

Alea felt a thrill; he had taken off the pack to free him for a fight. It was a good tactic, but what would happen if they stabbed at him?

"What did you say?" The leader's eyes narrowed.

Alea was wondering the same. What did the big galoot think he was doing? Didn't he know that kind of reaction would incite them to use those spears?

Yes, of course he did. Though why on earth he should be picking a fight with six mounted, armed men was more than she could say—until she remembered how much he could do with his mind.

"Hand it over, the sergeant said!" one of the men snapped.

"I'd rather not," Gar said.

"Then we'll take it!" The loudmouth drew back his spear.

"No, hold." The leader held up a hand, eyes narrowing. "What kind of man would talk back to six spears?"

"Someone who's big enough to carve up between us," another man grunted, leveling his weapon.

"And someone who's sure he can handle the lot of us," the sergeant said. "He can't, of course, but I'd like to know why he thinks so."

"The lot of us?" the other man scoffed. "He can't handle one!" He jabbed at Gar with his spear halfheartedly.

Gar whirled, the man yelped, and there was a loud crack.

3

Somehow Gar was standing with his back to a horse whose saddle was empty because its rider was struggling with Gar's arm around his neck, holding him as a shield.

"Yes, I thought it might be something like that," the leader said conversationally. "Good moves, fellow, but you don't really think you can take all six of us, do you?"

"I could have a lot of fun trying," Gar said with a grin.

The leader leaned back, looking down his nose at Gar with a weighing gaze. Then he nodded slowly. "A fighter like that, with a size like yours, would be just what the general wants. Gawn, take his pack."

One of the riders leaned down as his mount stepped forward and yanked at the pack. His eyes widened at the weight but he managed to swing it up in front of him anyway.

"There now," said the leader, "all this because you wouldn't give us your pack, and here we have it anyway."

"Only for the moment," Gar said.

"A bit more than that, I think," the leader returned, "but I'm not here for a few trinkets, I'm here recruiting. We'll let General Malachi bargain with you. Off up that track, big man, or we'll leave you here looking like one of your pincushions."

For a moment, Alea was afraid Gar was going to defy the man again—but he grinned and let the rider loose. "All right, I'll meet your general. He sounds as though he might be more of a match than this pollywog."

"Pollywog, am I?" the man husked, and coughed.

"Don't worry, your throat will be good as new within the hour," Gar assured him.

"You won't be, if I have anything to say about it! This pollywog has teeth!"

"Not until you've grown a bit."

The man mounted his horse, snarling, "This big enough for you?"

"Not really," Gar said. "Besides, I'll keep your tooth." He held up the spear.

The rider yanked a hatchet from his belt and swung it up.

"None of that!" the sergeant barked. "He's for the general!"

The rider froze, blood in his eye, then lowered his spear with a muttered obscenity.

"You shouldn't say such things about yourself," Gar admonished. He turned to the leader. "You take good care of your men."

"Meaning that even if we'd done for you, he wouldn't have seen the end of the fight?" The leader grinned. "We'll see how your boasts work in battle. What's your name, anyway?"

"Gar."

The leader didn't seem to notice the lack of a last name. "Well, Gar, I'm Sergeant Router, and you don't have your pack to guard your back anymore—so what say we all go to see General Malachi nice and friendly-like, eh?"

"Yes, I'd be very interested." Gar stepped forward into the middle of the group.

Most of the riders seemed a little taken aback at his sudden compliance, but Alea wasn't. She was sure that Gar was indeed very interested—interested in any hint of this planet's government, and a general would certainly be a good beginning for that. But why, in the name of Loki, had he baited them and earned their bad will if he was going to go with them anyway?

"Who gets his pack, Sergeant?" one of the riders asked.

"Drop it," Router said. "He'll be a soldier now, not a draft animal." He grinned down at Gar. "Of course, if you get away from us, you can always come back for it."

"Why should I want to get away?" Gar asked mildly.

"You'll learn the reason if the general lets you join up," Router said. "You'll be a soldier, my lad—that's what the general calls his men; he says it's an old word he's freshened up to use again. Yes, you'll be a soldier, and soldiers have to be trained."

One of the men gave a harsh laugh.

"General Malachi's idea of training can be kinda rough," another rider confided.

"I doubt I'll notice," Gar said. "Yes, by all means leave the pack, if you've no need of ribbons."

The riders all brayed laughter as though he'd made a hilarious joke and, still laughing, led him off down the road.

When they were well out of sight, Alea came out of the brush, hauled Gar's pack back in, and covered it with brambles and leaves, swearing at her companion's recklessness. She had no doubt he fully intended to come back for that pack—she would be very surprised if he decided to stay with this army.

What there was of the army, anyway. None of those riders had looked terribly professional. She certainly wouldn't have dignified any of them with the title of "soldier." Perhaps "bandits" or simply "outlaws," but they scarcely had the discipline she'd seen in the armies of her own people in Midgard, and certainly nowhere nearly as much as that of the dwarves.

She'd have to follow him, of course. If he had to fight his way free of an army, he'd need all the help he could get. She'd have to stay under cover, though—she wouldn't do him much good if she were caught before he made his break.

The patrol led Gar a mile down the road, then off to follow a deer trail that climbed higher and higher through the woods until it came out onto a sort of plateau that had been barricaded around with a fence made of brush. Looking more closely, Gar saw that the brush had long, sharp thorns. There was a sort of gateway blocked by two men holding long-handled axes. Gar frowned; there was something very amateurish about this army. They hadn't even invented proper halberds yet! Which meant their ancestors hadn't brought the knowledge from Terra and, in fact, had probably been careful to lose it.

"What's this, Router?" asked one of the guards with a nod toward Gar.

"A new recruit, boys, and one who's already proved he can fight a little," Sergeant Router said. "Let him in; we'll make sure he minds his manners."

The other guard guffawed and the first grinned. "I'm sure you will that! He's a big one, though, isn't he? Well, all the easier for the general to see. Take him in."

They rode through the gate and down a lane between brush huts, and other "soldiers" came out to gawk at the huge man striding between the horses; they called out some rude speculations about his ancestry. Since Gar didn't recognize most of the creatures involved, he declined comment.

In the center of the camp, they came to a larger hut that actually had wattle walls and a thatched roof. Three men were plastering the withes, but it still looked very temporary. In front of it stood a bull of a man a bit taller than the others, his leather tunic decorated with fringes and some brass ornaments. His hair was a black thatch, his eyes small but alert, his jaw square, and his nose crooked with a break that had healed wrong some years in the past. Near him, at various distances, stood men as big as himself, leaning on their spears with watchful eyes—a bodyguard, at a guess.

The bull-man's eyes glinted as he saw Gar in the midst of the patrol.

As they rode up to him, Router and his men held their hands to their brows, then away—very sloppy salutes.

The big man returned them, though, his gaze still on Gar. "What's this, Sergeant? A new recruit?"

"That he is, sir." Then to Gar, "Take your hat off when you're talking to your new general, man!"

Gar doffed his broad-brimmed hat, wondering when the general was going to feel rich enough to issue his men caps so they could take them off to show him respect. Until he did, he'd have to settle for the pantomime that constituted the salute.

"Found him strolling down the road, easy as you please, carrying a peddler's pack. Thought we'd find him a better task for a man."

"A man?" General Malachi curled his lip. "Any reason to think that's what he is, instead of one of these village sheep?"

"Well, he didn't want to take orders." Router grinned. "Thought he could take on all six of us. Had a bit of a dustup with one of my men. Handled himself pretty well, too."

"Might be worth his copper, then." Malachi turned to Gar. "What do you think of the army, man?"

"Soldiering is an ancient and honorable profession, sir."

"Honorable, is it?" Malachi grinned. "The folk of the three villages we've taken wouldn't say so. Still, it has a nice sound. So you came willingly, did you?"

"Yes, sir—once I had made it clear that coming to see you was my choice."

The riders muttered, exchanging uneasy looks.

Malachi nodded shrewdly. "Pulled one of 'em off his horse, did you? And warned the others you'd give him back in pieces if they tried to jump you, like enough." He transferred his gaze back to Router. "So you talked sweet reason to him, did you, Sergeant?"

"That I did, sir, and I do have to say he kept a civil tongue in his head when he answered me."

It was both a veiled boast and a statement that Router hadn't been overawed for a second, simply recognized talent when he saw it.

Malachi nodded. "Well, that's good enough to warrant a word or two. Bid your men take their ease for an hour, Sergeant, before you take them back on patrol."

Router hesitated, casting a wary glance at Gar.

"Leave him to us," one of the bodyguards said with a savage grin. "He won't touch the general, be sure of it."

"Nice to know you're thinking of my safety," General Malachi said with dry sarcasm, "but there's no need to worry, Sergeant. These men have stopped three assassins before now. No need to fear for me."

Really! The man had been more successful than Gar had realized, to have aroused such hatred. Gar wondered how the assassins had come even this close to him.

"Aye, sir." Router made his clumsy salute again and his men followed suit, then turned and followed him into the camp, muttering to one another. They seemed relieved, somehow.

General Malachi's voice turned to a bark. "Stand stiff, soldier! Know that you don't have any choice in this—you're one of my men now, like it or not, and your training sergeant will kick that into you till you don't dare talk back and do anything you're told instantly! It's going to be hell, learning to be a soldier, plowboy, and don't you think it won't be!"

"I'll make it through, sir," Gar said, "because I know when it's done, I'll be a soldier like—"

"Who asked you?" General Malachi's hand whipped out, slapping Gar backhanded. Pain slashed through his mouth and teeth and anger fought to erupt. He stood stiff as a board, keeping his hands at his side, throttling the anger.

Malachi stood watching him, fists on his hips, and his bodyguards stood taut and ready. When Gar stood firm, Malachi nodded, and the bodyguards relaxed ever so slightly. "Well," said the general, "you've learned the first rule of soldiering, and it came hard enough—but you learned it quick, I'll say that."

Gar, who had been a soldier and an officer in half a dozen armies, kept the contempt from showing in his face. The man was a rank amateur, but Gar wouldn't learn anything by saying so—and he had been suckered in neatly to that first "lesson."

"All right, then, you've learned," General Malachi said easily. "Anything you'd like to know? Don't worry, I'm giving you permission to speak now."

"Well, I was wondering, sir, how you became a general."

Malachi bellowed a laugh and his bodyguards snickered. "How I come to be a general? Why, I told the world I was, man, and defied it to tell me otherwise! Mind you, I started out as an outlaw like any, but I fought my way up to be captain of my band—and when I bludgeoned out another captain in fair fight and won his men, I decided I'd have to be more than a captain, so I thought through those old stories that only outlaws tell and remembered the ranks in the ancient armies. I called myself a major and dared any who thought otherwise to prove it on me. One captain dared, and after that I had three bands under me. Some others joined of their own choice, the rest I conquered, and when I bossed all the bands in this forest, I called myself colonel. Now that I've captured three towns, I think I rate the rank of general."

The bodyguards were nodding and grinning; Gar allowed himself a single thoughtful nod of his own. "Thank you."

"What about you?" Malachi's voice was a whip crack. "Think I don't deserve the title?"

"You have won it on your own terms," Gar said. He didn't add that by any real army's standards, Malachi wouldn't amount to more than a sergeant major, a lieutenant at the most.

"Well said." Malachi seemed to expand, preening. "Anything more you want to know before I hand you to a training sergeant who'll shove your face in the dirt?"

"Only wondering what you'll call yourself next."

"Why, king, of course," Malachi said with a grin that showed several broken teeth. "I aim to boss around everybody between the mountains to the east and the big river to the west, from the northern desert to the southern sea."

Ambitious, Gar thought, but had to put the idea in Malachi's idiom. "You don't think small, do you?"

"Well, we'll see." Malachi's grin widened. "Maybe when I've got the whole land, I'll think of something more."

The greed in his tone chilled Gar, but he only frowned as though puzzled and said, "It seems so plain when you say it that you make me wonder why nobody ever tried it before."

Malachi guffawed; his bodyguards joined in. Gar stood against their laughter with a look of polite inquiry.

"Ignorant enough, ain't he?" Malachi jeered, and the bodyguards chorused agreement. The biggest one said, "He's gotta be from so far out in the woods they still talk Bear!"

"I do come from far away," Gar acknowledged, "very far. I take it you're not the first to think of ruling the whole land, then?"

"Oh, there's plenty have," Malachi said. "No one knows how many—but none ever came anywhere near being king."

"Really?" Gar was extremely interested now. "These villagers don't look all that tough. What could stop a determined man?"

"Why, the Scarlet Company, of course!" Malachi said with scorn. "They've stopped every other man who wanted to be a king, but they won't stop me!"

The bodyguards gave a raucous cheer.

"Three of 'em have tried already," Malachi said, "and my bodyguards got 'em, every one!" He clapped the nearest man on the shoulder. "Ten of 'em there be, and every one as tough as oak! That right, Teak?"

"Right as reins, Gen'ral," Teak said with a gap-toothed grin. "Too bad they died so quick, though."

"Yeah, no chance to make 'em talk about the Company," Malachi grunted.

"Scarlet Company killers either die quick or talk quick," Teak complained. "Don't do no good either way."

"Maybe," Malachi growled, "but it does show that even the Scarlet Company can't stop me, not with you bravos watching."

"Be no loot and no women if you died, Gen'ral," Teak said. "I know it's best for you when my job's dull, but when it gets exciting, it gets really good." He pushed one fist into the other palm, squeezing and chuckling.

Gar gave the man a quick measuring look. Teak was the biggest of them, but he was still a head shorter than Gar. He made up for it in breadth, though—one solid block of muscle, under a layer of self-indulgent fat. Gar felt excitement stir—he hadn't had a good fight in a long time, too long, and Teak looked big enough to give him a challenge.

The bodyguard recognized the glint in his eye; his grin hardened. "Anytime, Longshanks. Any time."

"Why not now?" Gar asked.

Teak chuckled and stepped forward, but Malachi snapped, "None of that! When I'm in the mood to watch a fight, I'll let you know—but Teak's on duty and my bodyguards don't have any room to slack off!"

"Wouldn't call it slacking, Gen'ral," Teak said. "What do we know about him, eh? He could be a Company man, he could."

Malachi stared at Gar, startled by the thought. Then his eyes narrowed. "Yeah, I see what you mean. There's something about him, something wrong."

"The Gen'ral has the Second Sight sometimes," Teak explained to Gar. "It's one of the reasons he never loses, it is."

The other reason, Gar was sure, was because Malachi was always careful to attack antagonists who were weaker than he—victims, not foes.

"Yeah, there's something about him that could be my downfall," Malachi said with total certainty. "Don't know what it is, but it's there. Better not take chances."

Gar stared incredulously. His skin prickled as he realized that three of the bodyguards had drifted around behind him. He forced a laugh. "How's this? You don't fear the whole of the Scarlet Company, but one lone peddler is a danger?"

The general dismissed the objection with a chopping gesture. "You could be Company, like Teak says. I haven't conquered a forest and three villages by taking chances. Top him, Teak."

Teak stepped in with a gloating chuckle and a jabbing spear.

4

Gar stepped back, knocking the spear aside with one end of his staff, then swinging the other to clout the man on the side of the head. Teak gave a shout of surprise and pain and sank to his knees.

The other bodyguards bellowed and leaped in.

Gar fell. The three rushing behind him tripped over his body—pain ripped where they kicked—and fell into the three charging from the front.

The two at either side stepped in, jabbing downward with their spears and yelling in anger.

Gar swung his staff, knocking one's feet out from under him, then rolled to avoid the other three spears. One jabbed between his ankles, the other two behind him. He shoved himself up just as the fourth man fell on him, knocking him back into the earth; his spear point tore Gar's sleeve and pain flared in his arm. Gar swung a hard punch to the short ribs and the man's mouth gaped, eyes bulging, the wind knocked out of him. Gar shoved him aside and sprang to his feet.

But the six at front and back had sorted themselves out and turned on him. He backed away, staff whirling like a windmill. At least he had all of them in front of him now. They followed, wary and watchful.

General Malachi watched too, grinning, eyes bright, enjoying the show.

Two bodyguards stepped in, jabbing with their spears. Gar struck one with the full momentum of the whirling staff; it cracked across the spear shaft and the bodyguard howled with pain as it leaped out of his hands. With the rebound, Gar struck the other spear down. Its owner too bellowed with pain as the shaft kicked him in the ribs.

But they had bought time for the eight remaining to form a semicircle around Gar, backing him toward the trees, grins gone and eyes grim. There would be no more surprises; they were braced for a real fight. Gar retreated, staff still whirling as a shield between them and him, but felt his stomach sinking; six he might have managed, but nine?

Then he heard a voice call, "Lay off him!"

One man frowned and looked back at Malachi, calling, "What did you say, sir?"

"Me? Nothing!" Malachi scowled, surprised.

But the man had heard what Gar had. He hadn't known, though, that the voice was inside his head.

"Finish him off, Calaw!" Malachi shouted.

But another man turned to Calaw. "We should do *what?*"

"I didn't say anything," Calaw protested.

"Stab him!" Malachi howled.

Two more men looked up in surprise at something they

alone heard. Gar seized the moment and their spears—with his mind. The weapons twisted in their hands and thrust sideways at the five men who did step forward. They shouted in shock and anger and leaped away. "What the hell d'you think you're doing, fools?"

"We didn't," one of the men protested. "They just moved!"

Gar took two giant steps backward and felt leaves brush his back and sides, then close in front of him.

"Catch him! He's away!" shouted one of the other bodyguards and suited the action to the word.

With the baying of a hunting pack, the others leaped to follow.

A staff thrust out of the underbrush; two men tripped over it. It pulled back, then struck down to brain both. Three more, not seeing, charged toward Gar, thrusting, bumping into each other as they twisted to avoid tree trunks, then thrusting again. Gar sidestepped, caught one by the collar, and threw him into the other two.

Two more came plodding warily but quickly. The stranger's staff struck from behind and they fell.

For a moment, the way was clear as the conscious tried to sort themselves out and climb to their feet.

"Now!" Gar shouted, and turned to run zigzag between the trees. In two steps, Alea was at his side, glancing back with every step.

"Just listen to their thoughts," Gar told her. "Then you can spare your eyes for the road ahead!"

She matched him in twisting between trunks. The shouts behind them grew more distant. Soon only one pair of footsteps was crunching through the brush behind them.

Alea hurdled a log, then realized she was alone. She turned back in alarm, staff up to guard, and was just in time to see the lone bodyguard leap the fallen tree and tangle his legs on a staff that thrust up from behind the log as he landed. The man fell heavily and Alea didn't need a suggestion—she stepped in and brained him with her own staff.

"Nicely done," Gar said as he climbed to his feet, "and thanks for the help. Now let's run!"

When they reached the bottom of the hill, they slowed to alternate jogging with running.

"Why . . . isn't . . . anybody . . . following?" Alea asked.

"Read . . . them," Gar panted in answer.

Alea frowned, listening for thoughts as she ran. She heard satisfaction that the soldiers had chased away the intruder, along with chagrin that he had escaped—but overall, fear of the unknown that made them seek excuses not to follow Gar. Staves had, after all, twisted in hands, other staves had swung from hiding, and there was no way of telling how many companions Gar had with him. Worse, voices had called from nowhere. Not even Teak was overly eager to follow, so long as the suspect giant had been chased away.

"Nicely done, that," Gar said. "I didn't know you could project thoughts into other people's minds yet."

"Neither did I," Alea confessed, "but I had to try *some*thing!"

"Pretty good for a first try," Gar said dryly. "How did you imitate the different voices?"

Alea looked very confused. "I didn't."

"They filled that part in for themselves, then." Gar nodded. "Heard what they expected to hear. Well, part of it may have been luck, but it was still well and cleverly done—very well. Thanks for the rescue."

Alea glowed at the praise and scolded herself for letting it make any difference to her. She floundered for a minute, wondering how to respond, then realized that simplest was best.

"You're welcome." Then, with sudden chagrin at her interference, "What would you have done if I hadn't?"

"I hadn't quite figured that part out yet," Gar admitted.

Alea's spirits soared again, the aftermath of battle making her heady.

"What's General Malachi thinking?" Gar asked.

Alea bit back the retort that he could listen for himself. Of course he could, and probably was doing so even now—but he wanted her to practice. She concentrated on the welter of thoughts in the camp and picked out the flaring anger of the self-proclaimed general. Her eyes darkened with apprehension. "He's livid with rage," she said, "and giving orders for patrols to go out hunting us."

"Don't worry about them," Gar said. "Patrols will stick to the roads. No one is eager to come into the woods to chase us, and even if they did, their horses would slow them down; there are a lot of low branches here."

"But you're a marked man now. I hope you discovered a great deal in that camp, because we're surely not going to learn anything more after this!"

"I learned quite a bit, actually," Gar said thoughtfully, "mostly that there doesn't seem to be any government strong enough to keep this bandit captain from doing whatever he wants—except perhaps the Scarlet Company."

"Yes, I eavesdropped on your mind and heard them saying that." Alea frowned. "What is this 'Scarlet Company'?"

"Not a government, that's certain." Gar made a wry face. "I peeked in Malachi's mind, of course—he was enough of a bully that it seemed a good idea—but that didn't tell me anything more; all I had was a confused impression of blood and violence, and massive frustration that they stood in his way at all."

"How do they interfere, though?"

Gar shrugged. "By killing him, I guess—they've tried three times already. Since Malachi thinks bodyguards are the answer to the threat they pose, my guess is that this Scarlet Company is a band of assassins. I've heard of such things before—criminal organizations that kill people for hire. If Malachi has conquered half a dozen rival bands and three villages, I'm sure people are willing to spend their last penny to stop him."

"But you just said there wasn't any government strong enough to stop Malachi," Alea protested. "Why don't the governments just hire the Scarlet Company?"

Gar sat very still for a minute. Then he said, "You're right, of course. That's what they've done." He was silent another minute. "But that's just a guess. We'll have to go into one of the bigger towns, where the government must be, and make sure."

Alea frowned. "I thought this mission was over."

"Why should you think that?"

"Well . . ." Alea floundered, surprised that he didn't see the obvious. "They're hunting you now. How can we walk the roads if we have to keep hiding?"

"I'll travel in disguise, of course."

"Disguise! All seven feet of you? How will you disguise that?"

"By stooping," Gar said. "You'd be surprised how quickly I can age. I could be an old man of any kind; an ancient peddler with a heavy pack would have plenty of reason to stoop. Or I might be your crazy half-witted brother, cringing and fearful of everything about me—I've done that before, several times, and it's worked well. I don't think any of these troops will have the wit to guess how tall I would be if I stood straight. They're looking for a fighter, not a beggar."

"Well, it might work," Alea said doubtfully.

"I think we'd better make a few more miles through the woods before we try the roads again," Gar suggested. "And keep an open mind—open to hear other people's thoughts, that is. The patrols might try the forest, after all."

Alea hid a shudder as she stood. "They should be easy to lose in these trees." But she had memories of sleeping in branches and didn't want to repeat the experience.

A few hours later, she led Gar to their packs; she had hidden both when she went after him. Burdened again, they strode through the woods as quietly as possible.

As the forest darkened around them, Gar marveled that Alea's sullenness and anger seemed to have vanished with the landing. Perhaps it had just been cabin fever, after all.

On the other hand, there hadn't exactly been a great deal of time for an argument—and if she'd wanted a fight, she'd had a chance for a real one. He decided there was a great deal to be said for having common enemies.

They slept in the forest that night, and it was a cold camp with only a small and nearly smokeless fire.

"I'll take first watch," Gar offered.

"Why?" Alea demanded. "Because you don't think I can stay awake?"

Gar blinked in surprise. "Of course not. It's only that you're looking terribly tired."

"You're not looking terribly fresh yourself." It wasn't true, but he was probably feeling worn. "I suppose you think that I have to rest because I'm a weak woman."

"Scarcely weak, but very much a woman." Again, that brief flash of admiration that so irritated her. "Still, you should have the right to rest if you wish it."

"Oh, really? So that you can sit up and feel virtuous?"

"More to the point," Gar said, "so that I can meditate for a while.

I couldn't sleep, not yet. Too much has happened in one day."

"Don't you think I need some time to let the day's events sort themselves out?" Alea retorted.

Gar nodded slowly. "Then take it."

"Oh, so now I'm to sit up while you take your ease, am I? Shall I serve you breakfast, too?"

"Only if you take the second watch."

"So that's it! You want to wake up and find your food hot and ready, so you'll make me wake up in the middle of the night and start cooking!"

"Why don't we make it three watches tonight?" Gar sighed. "I'll take the first and the third, so I'll cook breakfast."

"So you can feel injured and nurture your resentment all night long? Not a chance! I'll take the first and the third!"

"Done," Gar said, "if they're each three hours long."

"And let you sleep six hours without an interruption? Just how selfish *are* you?"

"Incredibly," Gar said gravely, "selfish enough to want the first watch and the third so I can feel like a martyr."

"Well, it won't work!" Alea snapped. "*I'll* be the martyr, thank you! You can sleep and dream of me forcing myself to stay awake, pinching myself and holding my eyelids open!"

"You win." Gar sighed. "I'll take the first watch."

"Well, I should think you would!" Alea turned away, lay down, pulled up her blanket, and glared at Gar's back where he sat by the fire—legs crossed, back straight, hands on his knees, already meditating as he had said—and wondered why she felt as though she had lost.

Gar woke Alea in the middle of the night for her watch. She felt as though she were clawing her way up off a sheet covered with glue, but she fought off the yearning for the bed and pulled herself to her feet, then settled on a log by the fire.

Once she had moved that much, though, energy started to flow, and she didn't feel anywhere nearly as tired as she'd expected. Anger coiled; she suspected Gar had kept watch for the full six hours after all, letting her sleep—but she couldn't see the sky, so there was no way to tell time by the stars.

Alea eyed Gar covertly as he settled himself under his blanket and closed his eyes. When his breathing deepened in the slow rhythm of sleep, she turned to watch him openly. The man was an enigma to her, a puzzle that she despaired of solving. Her most spritely conversation, her tempers, her arguments, their verbal jousting—nothing could crack his shell, make him seem to care or to reveal anything about himself. Was she so ugly as to repel him, make him want to present only the blank public face he showed the rest of the world? If so, though, why had he invited her to come with him?

And why, in Loki's name, did he give her that admiring gaze now and then if he didn't want to do anything about it?

She sighed and turned away to scan the woods to the one side of the road, then the fields to the other. All other men were quite easy to understand—they wanted something, and you either gave it to them and let them go their way, or refused and endured their tempers or even, sometimes, their blows. Of course, since she'd met Gar, she'd learned to give as good as she got if a man tried to strike her—but that was another riddle about Gar: why would he teach her to fight when he knew it gave him that much less power over her?

Her gaze lingered on his sleeping form again; she forced it back to the woods. Of course, Gar was still far more skilled at fighting than she was, and much stronger—not that the last mattered; he had shown her how to use a man's strength and size against him. Still, he couldn't think of her as much of a threat.

Or much of a woman? If he had taught her men's skills, how feminine could he think her to be?

She absently noted the movement among the trees—an owl launching itself from a branch and skimming away to the fields, where it plunged. She looked out over the furrows, frowning and pondering. Apparently Gar didn't see her as being either feminine or a threat—so if he were to see her as a woman, would he feel a threat from something other than the blows of her staff? Certainly boys verging on manhood seemed to be afraid of the very femininity they desired. Was Gar still a boy in that sense?

She realized that her thoughts had begun to go in circles and gave up the puzzle with a sigh, turning back to scan the fields again, then the road and the woods—but the problem would not leave her alone, it kept nibbling at her mind. . . .

Then she saw the monster and the sight of it made her forget everything but its own grinning presence.

5

It was huge, easily her own height standing, which she discovered she was doing, staff raised to guard, words of alarm filling her mouth ready to be shouted. It might have been a cat, if a cat had had very short legs under a round body that swelled into a great ball of a head, making the whole creature seem to be only a vast face on top of furry feet, and a grinning mouth half that face, filled with nasty-looking triangular teeth that glinted in the firelight, very white, very sharp. The nose seemed only a nubbin and the eyes small, though each was at least the size of her hand, and they crinkled at the corners as if with amusement, making the toothy grin seem on the verge of laughing. But the ears atop the body were halves of a sphere, almost perfectly round.

Alea would have cried out, if the words hadn't purred in her mind:

Don't fear, woman. I shan't eat you.

What—what are you? Alea thought.

One of those who filled this planet before your kind came, the creature answered. Foolish folk, they think they slew us along with all the other animals that lived in this land before they came. We hide now, and they never see us—unless we want them to. Of course, no one ever believes those who do.

Then why show yourself to me?

Curiosity, the creature answered. You're not like the others, you and your mate.

He's not my mate!

You mean you don't know that yet? the creature asked. How foolish your kind are! Tell me, though, what was that great golden pie that dropped you like kittens from a mother's mouth?

The lie Gar had taught her sprang to her mind unbidden—but she looked in the creature's eyes, and the words stuck in her throat.

We know truth from falsehood, the creature told her, even if you do not. What was that thing—the wagon that brought you from the stars?

How—how did you know? Alea asked. Then anger came to her rescue. *If you knew, why did you ask?*

Because we have never seen one like it, the monster replied. The wagons that brought the ancestors of the people who live here, they were all ungainly, bumpy things that looked like very fat birds with very short wings. Its grin widened, and a drop of saliva dripped from a tooth. We eat birds.

Why don't you eat people? Alea demanded, fear gripping her vitals as her hands gripped her staff.

Because you have minds, the creature answered, minds complex enough to be aware of your own existence. In that, you are enough like us so that we could not think of you as food.

Even though these people took your land and chased you away?

There is surely enough land for us over the sea, if we wish it, the alien answered, unperturbed.

No, not alien, Alea realized—native. It was she who was the alien on this planet.

Even so, the monster agreed, but you are fascinating, and all the more so because you are alien. Those of us who grow weary of the daily round of hunting and eating and begetting and kit-rearing find diversion in the strange and foolish doings of your kind.

So you are glad to have them? Alea asked cautiously.

Quite pleased, the creature assured her, and you and your mate are even more diverting, because you are stranger than the strangers! You are new, you are novel, you are . . .

Not mates! Alea thought fiercely.

All kits must learn as they grow, the creature thought in a consoling tone. Be patient and you shall learn, too.

Alea stifled an angry comeback—it wouldn't do to antagonize a telepathic creature with so many sharp teeth. *Do you often show yourselves to the people? That must change the way they behave.*

It would indeed, the creature agreed, so we never let them see us—and if they should do so by accident, we make sure they forget. Still, there seem to be tales about us in the land.

Alea could believe that easily. *Why, then, do you show yourself now to me?*

To learn what you are, and what you mean to do, the creature said. Thus we showed ourselves to the first of your kind to come here, and would not let them settle until we were satisfied of their good intentions.

Alea frowned. *How did they convince you?*

By deciding to leave the planet as soon as they knew we were intelligent and self-aware, the creature replied. They trooped back aboard their bird-ships, and would have left, robbing us of a fascinating diversion.

So you told them they could stay?

We erased all memory of us from their mind, the creature told her. Then they had no reason to leave.

But they took your land!

We let them settle, the creature said. Those who did not find them amusing swam away to other lands. Those of us who loved to watch their antics retreated to the wild places, the barrens and the depths of the forests, the mountains and the fens, to listen to their thoughts and watch their mad caperings.

So now you come to see if I too shall be amusing, Alea thought, anger growing again.

More importantly, we wish to know your intentions toward our little friends, the monster thought. They have good hearts, most of them, and we would not like to see their lives disturbed.

We mean this land no harm, Alea said, *only good.*

I can see that in you, the creature replied. Moreover, I can see that you are very courageous—frightened, but able to overcome your fear. That is a brightness within you that we respect.

So—you do not object to our coming?

Be welcome, the monster thought. Help whom you can. If you need help yourself, remember and call upon me.

I—I thank you, Alea thought, astounded. *How—how shall I call?*

Call me "Evanescent," the creature replied. I shall come, or one much like me.

A sudden distant squalling off to her left made Alea turn to face it, staff coming up, heart pounding—but she recognized it even as it stopped: two cats disputing territory, or perhaps a coupling that one of them did not desire. She turned back to the fire, trying to make herself relax, wondering why she was gripping her staff so tightly. Really, a catfight was nothing to fear, and there hadn't been anything else to attract her attention, except that owl flying over the road—a very dull watch, in fact.

Sudden pain throbbed in her head, but was gone as quickly as the catfight. She pressed a hand to her temple, frowning. Something seemed to be missing there, some thought that she'd wanted to remember but that had slipped away. Well, she had much to learn yet, about meditation.

She scanned the woods again, then the fields, seeing nothing unusual—but she did notice that the gloom had lessened. She stood and stretched, amazed at how quickly the night had passed, amazed that dawn was coming and it was time to start cooking breakfast. *That* would teach Gar to let her sleep longer than she deserved!

Still, she would have liked to remember that fleeting thought. Well, if it was important, it would come back to her.

The next day, Gar stripped down to his breechcloth and folded his clothes carefully, then smeared himself liberally with dirt, mixing dead grass and leaves into his hair while Alea packed his clothes under her trade goods.

"How's this?" Gar hunched over, even bending his legs, and stumbled toward her, whimpering, "Poor Gar's a-cold! Poor Gar's a-cold!"

"I should say you are." Alea stared, unnerved by the change in his appearance; surely she would never have recognized him through all that dirt. He was right—bent over like that, he actually seemed shorter than she was. *Which isn't saying much,* she thought with irony. She was well over six feet herself, after all, and had long ago resigned herself to never finding a husband—and still didn't think to, but here she was traveling with a man who actually made her feel small! "How are you going to keep from freezing?"

"I'll grow used to it," Gar assured her. "If worse comes to worst, we can trade for a blanket at the next village."

So off they went at sunrise, Gar slouching along at her side, which took a foot off his height. "If we hear a patrol," he assured her, "I'll cringe low again."

"Let's hope they don't throw water on you," Alea said.

Gar stopped and frowned up at her. "I don't have the right to pull you into danger with me—and you're right, there's far too much chance of our being discovered. Perhaps we should abort the mission after all—I have no right to put you in danger just to satisfy my insatiable curiosity."

Privately, Alea agreed, but aloud she only said, "Don't be ridiculous!"

They found a village late in the afternoon and came out onto the road so that they would seem to be normal travelers. Gar started cringing well before they came in sight of the houses.

It was a tidy place, prosperous though not rich—a circle of wattle-and-daub cottages with thatched roofs and plain shuttered openings for windows. Flowers made the patches of lawn colorful; chickens scratched behind the houses between fences that separated them from the family pigs.

They had arrived at a good time; people were coming in from the fields. They turned to the travelers with cries of welcome.

"Hail, strangers!"

"Peddlers! Have you ribbons?"

"Good evening to you! What news of the wide world?"

Thus they came into town in the center of an ever-growing crowd, none of whom seemed put off in the slightest by Gar's disguise. Alea was a little dazed by all the fuss, especially since she hadn't worked much at screening out others' thoughts yet—on a ship between stars, there hadn't been the need. Now, though, she was finding that having learned to open her mind to hear others' thoughts didn't necessarily mean she could close it again at will.

Gar could, though. With the ease of long experience he looked up at the people with a loose-lipped grin, waving and chirping, "Lo! Hi! Goo'morn!"

"Hey, it's an idiot!" one teenage boy called to his friends. "This could be fun!" They started toward Gar.

Alea stiffened with alarm—but a middle-aged man interposed himself smoothly between Gar and the boys and said, "Now, lads, that's not kind. Would you want someone to make a mock of you?"

The boys glowered at the rebuke. One said, "I'd like to see them try!"

"I wouldn't," the man said and nodded at Gar. "Look at the size of those shoulders, the thickness of those arms! Feeble his mind may be, but not his body. He seems gentle enough, mind you, but I wouldn't want him angry with me."

The boys turned thoughtful at that and held back, letting others move near the couple first—and when they did speak to Gar later, Alea noticed they were almost kind in their talk.

She pulled herself together and imitated Gar's greetings, though with rather better speech, calling replies to as many as she could. The welcomes died down as they came into the common, the circle of grass between the cottages, and one woman thrust her way to the fore, calling, "What have you in your packs, goodfolk?"

"Aye!" cried a middle-aged man. "What have you to trade?"

Gar swung his pack off his back, and his voice spoke in Alea's mind. "*'Trade,' not 'sell.' Interesting.*"

We'd better not use coins. Alea was unnerved by the contrast between his half-witted grin and his analytical thoughts.

Perhaps one, just to see if they know what coins are.

Alea didn't answer, only swung her pack down, then loosened the buckles and opened the flap. The people crowded round with cries of delight.

Not much to do in this town, Gar thought wryly. Alea's lips pressed tight to hold back laughter, and he knew she had "heard." It also seemed to relax her, as he'd hoped it would. After all, if they were the most exciting thing to happen all week, life must be very . . . placid.

"The poor lad!" said one kindly-looking grandmotherly woman. "Well, we've seen enough of his kind to know he's no danger."

Inbreeding! Gar thought, then chirped, "Poor Gar's a-cold! Poor Gar's a-cold!"

"As surely he must be," a younger woman said sympathetically. "Have you no clothes for him, lass?"

"I have, though sometimes he can't stand the feel of them and tears them off," Alea ad-libbed, and was amazed at her own glibness. "Have you a blanket? I could trade you, say . . ." She let the sentence trail off, and the younger woman picked up the hint, eyes gleaming. "A small pot, perhaps?"

Alea reached into her pack. "Iron or copper?"

"What—would you take a blanket for a copper pot?" the woman asked, her eyes round.

Alea realized she'd named too low a price. "It's very thin copper," she said apologetically, "easily dented."

"Oh! Well, a blanket of my thickest weave would be worth an iron pot." The woman eyed her warily, though.

Still too high a price. "Throw in dinner and a night's lodging, and you shall have it."

"Done!" the woman cried. "I'll fetch the blanket." She turned and hurried off to her cottage.

"I'll have a pot, too!" The middle-aged woman held out a necklace.

It seemed only a string of polished quartz pebbles to Alea, but Gar caught his breath and Alea heard his thought: *Diamonds!*

The kindly woman mistook his fascination and smiled, twisting the string this way and that so that the light twinkled off the surfaces. "Aye, 'tis a pretty thing, is it not? Buy it, my dear, if only to please your friend."

"Not only my friend, but my brother, too," Alea corrected.

"Brother? Aye, you're both quite tall, aren't you? Well, it's a good woman you are to take care of a sib so afflicted." The woman held out the necklace. "Here, take it and a blessing on you both. I can find many more."

"No, no!" Alea protested, and pulled a copper pot out of her pack. "Here, take it! If the metal's not too thin for you, that is."

The woman handed her the necklace and took the pot. She pursed her lips, weighing it in her hand and rubbing the metal between her fingers. "Not so thin as all that. I doubt not it will make a good kettle for boiling water."

"Oh, well, if you want a real kettle, I've that too." Alea pulled a small copper teakettle from Gar's pack. Several people gasped at the brightness of it, then started bidding.

Alea did brisk business, exchanging trade goods for rough gems and exquisite pottery that would sell well in the next village. In some cases, she had nothing that the people wanted, but there were little wedges of copper and silver in her pack, and the villagers were quite happy to take those for their porcelains.

In the middle of it, a teenage girl pushed through to her, holding out a wide and beautifully embroidered belt. "What will you give me for this? I want sweet-smelling perfume and pretty things to wear!"

Alea stared at the belt. "I've nothing as pretty as that."

"Aye, Renga, that took me weeks to fashion for you." The older woman who came up beside her looked troubled.

"You gave it to me!" Renga snapped. "It's mine to do with as I wish!"

"It is," her mother said, "but it has my love and care stitched into it with the pattern. The day will come when you'll treasure that."

"You can't make me keep it!"

"No, I can't and I won't." Her mother sighed. "But it does

hurt me that you could think of trading it for a bit of shiny brass. Precious things should be saved, or you'll have nothing when you're old."

Renga hesitated, startled at the thought of the future, and Alea took the chance to reinforce what her mother had said. "A girdle like that takes a great deal of time and skill in the making, lass. My mother made me several such ornaments, and I treasured them even then—but much, much more when they were taken from me." The memory brought tears to her eyes, but she blinked them away angrily. "She's gone now, and I dearly wish I had something of hers to make me feel close to her still."

Renga stared, shocked, then held out her girdle in sympathy. "Oh, take mine, then! I still have a mother, thank the Goddess! If this will help your heart, take it!"

Her mother looked startled, then slowly smiled and gazed at her with pride.

"I thank you, lass, and it's good of you to offer," Alea said gently, "and a treasure it is—but it was made by your mother, not mine, and would only remind me of my loss, not be a part of my mother to comfort me." She smiled and pressed the girl's hand. "But your care cheers me more than you can know. Here, take this of me for thanks." She pressed a small ring into the girl's hand.

Renga looked down at it and gasped with delight, then forced herself to hold it out. "I thank you deeply, mum, but it would be wrong to take it and give nothing in return."

"Why, then, give me a gift," Alea said, smiling, "whatever you choose—but I will say that my brother and I grow hungry on the road."

"Bread of my own baking, and cheese then!" Renga turned to hurry back to her family's cottage.

"You have every reason to be proud," Alea told her mother.

The woman turned back from beaming fondly after the girl. “I am that, lass, and I thank you.” She shook herself, becoming businesslike again. “But a daughter like that deserves a pretty or two. I’ve opals and garnets to trade; have you a necklace to match that ring?”

Alea dug in her pack, back to business again.

When the customers were done with her, they went to listen to Gar, who had taken out a wooden flute and was drawing a mournful tune from it. When he was finished, a man said, “Witless or not, you’ve some talent, lad.”

Gar nodded wisely and said, “Talent is governance.”

Several people smothered laughter, but the man only smiled with sympathy and asked, “Governance? What’s that, lad?”

“Order,” Gar said, and blew a scale, then looked up, grinning. “Order.”

“Setting the notes one after another, eh?” The man nodded, considering.

“Order chickens,” Gar suggested. “Order houses.”

“Housework, you mean? No, that’s economics,” said a middle-aged woman.

So it was, Alea remembered—the Greek word had originally meant wise and thrifty household management.

“Many houses!” Gar spread his hands wide to embrace the whole village. “Who orders you?”

Now they all laughed. Gar stared, startled and frightened. Seeing that, the villagers choked off their laughter and the man explained, “It’s a comical notion, lad, one person ordering the whole village.”

“Why, we can make all the order we need by ourselves,” the woman said, “each tending to her own house and garden.”

“And all of us tending the crops in the fields,” another man agreed, "children to watch the sheep crop the lawn, and us to watch the children. What more order does anyone need?"

Gar looked up at them wide-eyed, then glanced over each shoulder apprehensively and beckoned the man closer. With a gentle smile, the man complied, and Gar whispered into his ear, "Bandits!"

No one laughed this time and the man said gravely, "Ah, bandits there are—for those who want what others have, and who won't care for their own house and garden, can't stay in the town. Then they band together and come to try to take what we have. But if they become too big a nuisance, the Scarlet Company stops them, of course."

By this time, everyone was done trading and had gathered around Gar. Alea buckled their packs and came into the circle, saying, "You mustn't mind his silly questions, good people. He can't remember the answers, so he asks them again in every village."

"It's good of you to say so, lass," said a grandmotherly woman, "but such questioning is as much to be expected of an idiot as of a little child. We must be kind to all."

Alea sighed. "Sometimes I am amazed and delighted at the goodness of people."

Gar exchanged a quick and piercing glance with her; he too was amazed at the gentleness and understanding of these villagers. Then he turned back to the people with a gaze once more vacant and tried again. "Who gives orders?"

"Why, everyone will order what they want from your sister, lad," the grandmother told him, "and if she has it, we will bargain with what we have."

Gar surrendered and only gave them his loose-lipped grin while he pulled the coarse, brightly patterned blanket closely around him. "Gar's not a-cold anymore!"

The people laughed again, more with pleasure at seeing him warm than in ridicule.

At last they apologized for lack of hospitality but said they had a day's work to do and drifted away to evening chores and back into houses—but the woman who had traded a night's hospitality brought them hot porridge, saying, "I don't know when you ate last or how much, but I'll warrant it was hours past. Eat of this; it should go well with Renga's fresh bread and cheese."

Surprized and gratified, Alea said, "Thank you kindly, good woman—very kindly indeed!"

"Thank kindly!" Gar agreed.

"It's my pleasure," the woman said, smiling at the thanks, "and part of my bargain, after all. My name is Llyena, by the way. If you feel like telling tales or singing songs to keep the little ones busy, that would be kind. We'll all hope to hear news from you after supper." Her eyes turned almost avaricious, but when Alea didn't offer any sudden disclosures, she smiled, nodded at them, and went back to her garden.

"We had better think up some news quickly," Gar muttered.

"Long-distance listening is your job." Alea gave him a slab of bread and cheese. "I'm too new at telepathy. I can tell them about General Malachi, though."

"That should do for a start," Gar agreed. "Still, the telepathy might yield some results."

"You mean you haven't tried it yet?"

"Well, yes, while I was keeping watch last night," Gar confessed, "though people's dreams aren't exactly sound journalistic sources." He frowned. "Frustrating, too—no one was dreaming anything about the government."

"Would you expect them to?" Alea demanded.

"Well, there's usually someone having nightmares about

taxes," Gar replied, "and someone dreaming about being a king or a queen—but there was none of that here."

Alea shrugged. "Maybe they don't have kings and queens. My people didn't."

"Yes, but you did have squires, and they had a council. No one here was dreaming about anything of the sort—except the bandits."

"They don't have to have a government," Alea pointed out.

"Ridiculous!" Gar scoffed. "Every society has to have a government of some sort. Without it, a nation falls apart. That's what happened to the cultures who did try it, and that's why they're not around anymore."

"People can always discuss their problems over a campfire or a banquet table," Alea protested.

"Yes, but that's called a village council, and it's a government of a sort," Gar said. "Admittedly, it's pretty minimal, and it won't work for anything larger than a village. Have a city or even a dozen villages, and you have to have a formal council that meets regularly. Then some people will emerge as leaders in that council, and you'll start having officials of one sort or another."

"Perhaps that's all they have here," Alea offered.

"I'd settle for it," Gar said, "but I haven't seen any sign of it, either in people's dreams last night or among our customers today."

"You were studying them," Alea accused.

"Of course," Gar said. "I wasn't about to ignore them, after all—but I didn't see any sign of a power structure at all!" He sounded very frustrated.

Alea hid a smile and said, "Well, I did notice that the adults deferred to their elders. The youngsters were pretty good about that, too, but they had lapses."

"Teenagers always do." Gar shuddered at a flash of memory from his own adolescence. "Respectful and defiant by turns."

"It's part of growing up," Alea agreed, "but these adults are very gentle about restraining their young people."

"Very," Gar agreed, "and the kids seem to respond to it." He looked up with his loose-lipped grin as a woman passed by carrying a basket. She paused at a post set at the edge of the common and dropped something into a box fixed to its top, then went her way.

"What did she drop in there?" Gar's gaze was glued to the box.

"I saw the flash of metal," Alea said.

"So did I." Gar frowned. "You don't suppose it was one of Herkimer's little copper trade wedges, do you?"

"It seems likely," Alea said. "I suppose these people even have a way of collecting to help their poor."

"A good thought," Gar said, "but I don't see any poor—unless you want to count them all, but if they're poor, they certainly don't realize it."

"A religious offering?" Alea guessed.

"That makes sense." Gar nodded, brooding. "Drat it! That's going to plague me until I know the answer for certain now!"

"Maybe we can ask over dinner," Alea suggested. "I'll see if I can work it into the conversation."

"Good luck," Gar said dryly. Then he let his face relax into the very picture of good-natured idiocy. "Here come customers."

Alea looked up and saw half a dozen children running toward her. She smiled and sat, spreading her skirts, and gesturing to them to do likewise. Beside her, Gar started playing his flute.

The children came to a halt, wide-eyed and curious. The biggest girl said, "Could you tell us a story?"

"I'd be glad to," Alea said, and gestured at the grass. "Sit down, then, and listen."

The children sat. Two women and a man looked up and saw, and came strolling over to listen, too.

"Long ago and far away," Alea began, as tradition dictated. "there was a land watched over by gods who lived in a magical kingdom in the sky, called Asgard. The king of those gods was called Odin, and . . . yes?"

One of the children had raised a hand. Now she asked, "What's a king?"

6

Well . . ." Alea paused, taken aback, then said, "A king is a man who gives orders to everyone else."

"Why?" one of the children asked.

Alea tried to think of a good reason, but could only say, "Because he doesn't have anything else to do. Besides, all the other gods were Odin's children, so they paid attention to what he said."

"Oh," the child said, thinking it over. Then, "Did he have a lot of children?"

"Lots and lots," Alea said. "But this story is about one of his sons, the thunder god, and his name was Thor—and Thor had a friend named Loki."

The adults frowned, and one of the children said, "Three boy gods? Isn't that too many?"

"Why, how many should there be?" Alea asked in surprize.

"Well, one boy god in the sky and one girl god in the earth is enough," the child answered, and the adults nodded.

"Oh," Alea said, and thought fast. "Well, this story was made up a long, long time ago, before people realized that. They still thought there were lots and lots of gods and goddesses. Anyway, one morning, Thor woke up and . . ."

"Didn't Thor have a mommy?" asked one little girl.

"A mother?" Alea asked, startled. "Well, of course he did—Odin's wife, Freya. But she isn't part of this story."

"Why not?" asked a big boy. "Mothers are important!"

"Why, so they are, and I know other stories about Freya and the goddesses of Asgard," Alea said, surprised. "Would you rather hear one of those?"

"What's this story about?" asked a five-year-old.

"It's about Thor's visit to Jotunheim, the land of the giants," Alea said.

A chorus of "ooohs" answered her, and several voices said, "Let's hear about the giants!"

"Well, then." Alea recovered her composure. "One morning, Thor woke up and found his magic hammer, Mjollnir, missing. He asked all around, but nobody had seen it. The watchman of the gods, though, had seen a giant sneaking around, and that's how they realized that one of the giants had stolen Mjollnir."

"What's 'stolen' mean?" asked a little girl.

Alea stared a moment, then said, "Taking something that belongs to someone else, without asking."

"Oooooh!" said several voices, and, "That was naughty!" said another.

"Naughty indeed." One of the parents frowned. "Surely the other people who lived in this Asgard banded together to make the giant give back the hammer!"

"No," said Alea, "because he lived with the other giants, in their own land. They were people of completely different nations, not just a different village."

"Even so! The giant villagers would have made the thief give it back!"

"No," said the grandmother. "Perhaps they didn't know one of their number had taken it."

"Oh, they knew," Alea said rashly, "and were proud of it."

"Well! I never!" a mother huffed.

Alea realized that was probably true.

"What horrid people, to be proud of such a thing!" said a father.

"What monstrous sort of people were these giants, who would applaud a thief?" asked a third parent.

Alea saw a mother glancing with concern at her children and caught her feelings of apprehension. The man beside her was looking at her and Gar as though wondering whether or not to run them out of town. Could this story really be so controversial that the parents thought it was dangerous for their children?

Yes—if they had never heard of stealing, and if all villages were friendly with one another. Who would want the ideas of theft and war introduced where they hadn't been?

"But what difference did it make?" asked an older man in a reasonable tone. "Couldn't this Thor have just shrugged and made himself another hammer?"

"Well, it was a magical hammer," Alea said. "Anytime he threw it"—she barely managed to keep herself from saying "at somebody"—"it came flying back to him."

The children ooohed again, eyes round with wonder, but one of the fathers asked. "Why would he need a hammer that came back to him? Was he so lazy that he couldn't go pick it up? And why would he want to throw it, anyway?"

Alea started to tell him the hammer was a weapon of battle, but out of the corner of her eye she saw Gar shake his head a centimeter, and Alea remembered that these people might not have heard of war. She glanced at the other parents; she had learned enough of telepathy to be able to perceive their growing unease at such an unfit tale, so she made some quick changes. "It was a special hammer, for hunting," she said, making it up on the spot. "His people thought it was more merciful to knock animals senseless than to let them feel the pain of arrows or spears."

"How kind!" a woman exclaimed, and the men nodded judiciously. One said, "A hammer that came back could be very useful in the forest, where a tool could easily be lost in the underbrush."

"Or fallen into a lake, if you were shooting geese," another man agreed. "Yes, that could be quite valuable. Odd thing for a hunt, though."

Another man shrugged. "We use boomerangs for much the same purpose. Was his hammer some sort of boomerang, lass?"

"Something like that," Alea said, relieved. "The gods valued it highly, so Odin sent Loki and Thor to make the giants give back Mjollnir."

The older woman shook her head in disapproval. "To think that he could give orders to another adult!"

"A fool," one of the men opined. "When a child's grown, he should still consider his elder's words carefully, but that doesn't mean he has to obey them if he doesn't think them wise."

"Odin had no business trying to give orders to another adult," said another, and there was a general chorus of agreement.

"Odin *was* Thor's father," Alea reminded.

One of the younger mothers frowned at her. "Do you come from a land where the parents think they can go on bossing their children all their lives?"

Yes, Alea thought, remembering her neighbors—but she remembered her own gentle parents, too, whom the neighbors scolded for not laying down the law to Alea, and how deeply she missed them now that they were dead. She choked back the tears and said only, "It was their custom."

"A bad one," one of the men said severely. "God or not, I think that perhaps Odin was a very bad father."

Alea was astonished to find that she agreed with him.

Another woman asked, "Didn't Thor's mother have anything to say about this trip?"

Lamely, Alea had to admit, "She didn't have much to do with Thor after he became a teenager."

All the people shook their heads, adults and children alike exclaiming at the scandal. One childish treble rose clearly above all: "Poor man!"

"Poor indeed!" the older woman said, seeming shaken. "What an undutiful son, what a neglectful mother!"

"The one follows from the other, I suppose, Aunt," one of the younger women said. "If she neglected him so, it's no wonder he didn't pay any attention to her when he was grown."

The parents nodded, agreeing with her in many different words but one common opinion.

"Well, Thor was eager for more traveling, anyway," Alea said quickly. Out of the corner of her eye, she saw Gar sitting with his head bowed, lips pressed tight and shoulders shaking.

"Wasn't one *wanderjahr* enough for him?" the younger woman said, frowning.

"No, he was like us peddlers," Alea said, "one of the ones who has a great deal of trouble settling down."

"Well, he was the thunder god, she said, and storms do travel," a man said thoughtfully. "If they didn't, one village would be drowned while another was parched. I suppose a thunder god would have to be a wanderer, yes."

"That was it!" Alea said, relieved. "So he and Loki harnessed

Thor's two giant goats to his chariot and drove away down the road toward Jotunheim."

"Giant goats?" one of the children asked, eyes wide.

"Oh yes, taller than a man at the shoulders," Alea said, warming to her audience, "with long twisted horns and shaggy black-and-white coats. Thor's chariot stood on wheels as tall as my shoulder and rose as high as the goats' horns. What was more, those goats could fly and pull the chariot through the air faster than any bird."

"Magic indeed," one of the parents said above the children's excited murmurs.

"Well, he had to be able to fly, to bring the storms," Alea explained, then looked down at the children. "Do you know, when the lightning flashes, how there's a big boom, then a rumble dying away? That boom is the sound of Mjollnir hitting a cloud, striking the gigantic sparks that we call lightning. The rumble is Thor's chariot wheels rolling away across the sky."

The children chorused wonder, and the parents smiled, recognizing a fairy story when they heard one.

Encouraged, Alea went on to tell her audience how Thor and Loki had decided they would have to camp at the end of the day and came down to earth to find a cave taller than Thor's head, which wasn't exactly a cavern but was warm and dry inside. There were five smaller caves arranged around the outside, but they were too narrow to be interesting, so Thor and Loki ignored them. The children shivered with delicious apprehension, wondering what would come out of such horrid places, and were rather disappointed when nothing happened all that night. But when a giant came the next morning to invite Thor and Loki to his hall, then picked up the "cave" and slipped it on his hand, the children laughed and clapped, delighted that the giant's glove could be so huge that the gods would have been able to spend the night in it.

"What happened when they came to the giant's hall?" one of the boys asked, eyes shining.

But Alea had been smelling dinner cooking for some time and the parents were glancing at the cottages and beginning to look impatient. "Perhaps I'll tell you that after dinner," she said, "but I'm rather tired of talking now."

The children complained, a disappointed chorus, but the older woman stepped forward to clasp Alea's shoulder with a friendly touch, saying, "You're rather hungry, too, I should think, lass, and if you're not, your brother must be, with a great frame like that to fill! No, children, she has the right of it—we'll come out to the common after dinner, if she is willing, but for now, it's time for supper."

Disappointed but hopeful, several children went home with each adult. Alea was interested to see that every man or woman went to a different cottage; apparently there had been no adult couples here, which meant that men as well as women did the cooking, just as women worked alongside the men in the fields. She marveled at the notion, delighted, but wondered how they decided who did which chore.

Over dinner, the parents with whom they were staying let her know, very gently, their concerns about the moral values in the tale she'd been telling. Alea assured them the rest of the story was nothing to distress them, and sure enough, after dinner, she presented the tale of the giants' challenge as a friendly invitation to a contest, and the theft of Mjollnir had been only a practical joke designed to bring the strongest god and the shrewdest god to match strength, speed, and wits with the giants, simply to while away a dull winter's day. In that context, everybody could relax and enjoy the eating bout and the race and the feats of strength—and rather than recapturing Mjollnir and using it to lay waste the giants' hall, Thor was awarded his hammer as a prize and sent on his way back to Asgard with good wishes. The tale ended with giant and god in happy accord, and the audience loved the tale. Alea was rather impressed with it herself, in spite of the fact that Gar refused to meet her eyes and kept his thoughts shielded.

The children pestered Alea for another story, of course, but the parents firmly sent them off to bed, claiming the peddlers must be exhausted with so much talking, then turning to Alea with avid interest as the children scampered away, asking, "What news have you of the wide world?"

"Nothing terribly much." Alea's thoughts raced. "Someone claimed to have seen a great golden disk in the sky some days ago."

The people laughed and one man asked, "How much had he been drinking? I wonder."

"Oh, I saw a disk in the sky myself," one of the women said. "I call it 'the sun.' "

They laughed anew at that, then quieted, looking hungrily to Alea.

"There is General Malachi," she said tentatively.

The people's faces darkened. "General, is it?" said an older man. "It was 'major' when last we'd heard, and that just means 'bigger.' What does 'general' mean, I wonder?"

"Including everything," Alea said, "which I gather is what Malachi means to do. He has conquered all the outlaw bands in his forest and seized three villages around the woods."

The people were startled and unnerved. "Seized them? What did he do with them?" one woman cried.

"Plundered and bullied, I don't doubt," the oldest man

said, his bushy white brows drawn down so far as to hide his eyes in shadow. "I've seen the like of him come, and I've seen them all go, or heard of it. But they cause a deal of grief while they last."

"Bandits always do," a woman agreed. "I suppose we'll have to band together with the other villages soon to go and talk sense into them again."

"The only talk they'll listen to is the sound of scythes and flails." The old man sighed. "Still, we must see the roads safe for the bands of young folk in their *wanderjahrs.*"

"You had best do it quickly, then," Alea said, "before General Malachi becomes too strong. He's making the people of the captured villages fight for him."

That upset the villagers mightily. They burst into talk, but not arguing about the best way to counter General Malachi—only deploring what he was doing, and wondering how a decent human being could do such things. The consensus, of course, was that he wasn't decent at all—but someone said sagely, "Well, the Scarlet Company will do for him," and everyone else agreed, their faces clearing, as they nodded and said in many words how they could leave General Malachi to the Scarlet Company.

As their hosts led them back to their cottage, Gar noticed a man stopping by the box on the post—but it wasn't a bit of copper he dropped in, it was a white chip of wood with some marks on it. Gar listened to his thoughts and was surprised to feel the man's satisfaction at that overbearing Orlo having his comeuppance. Intrigued, Gar wished he could stay to see who emptied the box.

When the cottage was quiet and Alea and Gar lay on opposite sides of the hearth on pallets of clean straw covered with sheepskins, she thought as clearly as she could,

What else was I supposed to do, then? I had to make the story one they would accept!

You did beautifully, Gar assured her, *and pardon my laughter. It was a most amazing transformation. I can hardly wait to hear your version of Ragnorak.*

Alea felt a bit better about it. She told herself it was only because such an exchange of thoughts was a useful exercise in telepathy; she had practiced daily with Gar aboard ship, but this was a very different order of things indeed.

No doubt I shall have Heimdall play his horn for a dance, and have Tyr teach the Fenris Wolf to sit up and shake paws. Alea's thought had a sardonic overtone. *Still, I cannot help but wonder what sort of land this is if they do not know what theft is, nor wish to hear of strife between two villages.*

A pleasant relief from most of the worlds I have visited, Gar thought. *One grows tired of bloodshed—very tired indeed. But what do you make of their insistence that Odin had no right to give orders to Thor, once he was grown?*

I rather agree with it, Alea thought back, *and even more with the notion that Freya had as much business being in the story as Odin. I would guess these people are pagans of a sort, but rather more efficient about it than my own people.*

If they are content with only one god and one goddess, certainly, Gar thought back. *Of course, the irreverent might say they were too poor to afford more.*

Irreverent indeed! Alea thought indignantly. *I will be interested in learning more about their religion. From what I've seen here, I would guess the god and goddess are evenly matched. Did you notice that both men and women tilled the fields, and both seemed to prepare dinner?*

I did notice, Gar thought. *Perhaps they're doing something radical, such as deciding that the one who has more talent for cooking should prepare the meals.*

Or perhaps they simply take turns! Alea snapped in return, then wondered why his statement irritated her.

Quite possibly, Gar agreed. *In any event, if they believe parents should not command their children once they are grown and think men and women should be equal in authority, I cannot help but think this is a most astonishingly egalitarian society.*

If there is a government, Alea said, *it is a government of equals.*

That is, at least, the theory of democracy, Gar said, *though if these people have a central government over all the villages, I certainly saw no sign of it today.*

Well, when they've never heard of a king and think it odd that someone would give orders to others, I would doubt they have any government at all.

There must be one somewhere, Gar thought, and Alea peered between her lashes to see his face screwed up in concentration. *No society can survive without a government.*

A village can, Alea reminded him, *only a hundred people or so. When everyone knows everyone else, they need only sit around and talk over their issues.*

Yes! A government! Gar exulted. *A town council!*

Alea smiled, amused. *Well, if that's all you need, I'm sure you'll find many of them in this land.*

I would like something a bit more elaborate, Gar confessed.

But what of the bandits? Alea frowned. *Don't these people understand how much of a threat General Malachi is?*

They seem to be quite content to leave him to the Scarlet Company, whatever and whoever it is, Gar thought grimly. *I just hope he doesn't do too much damage before they learn otherwise.*

Alea shuddered and forced her thoughts into less troubling channels. *Odd that these people don't think of the bandits as stealing.*

No, Gar agreed. *When a bandit does it, they call it plundering, and I suppose that* is *different from one of your fellow villagers taking something that belongs to you.*

And when bandits fight villagers, they call it bullying. Alea mused. *True enough, but I think it misses the horror of what a band of brutes like that can do.*

May their god and goddess grant they never learn!

I think we may have to take a hand with that, Alea answered. *Who knows? Perhaps we only* thought *it was our idea to come here at this time.*

Perhaps so. But Gar's tone was amused. *All we can do is try to achieve harmony with whatever Power there is and trust that we will act as it wishes.*

Alea frowned, wondering if he was mocking her—but there was too much sincerity behind the terms he used and too much uncertainty as to what form that Power took. A mocker would have given them a name and form to lampoon.

Somewhat reassured, she settled herself for sleep and thought, *Well, perhaps we can't do anything about it, but talking makes the troubles seem smaller.*

A problem shared is a problem halved, Gar agreed. *Good night, Alea.*

Good night, Gar. Alea smiled as she curled a little tighter on her pallet and, before sleep claimed her, wondered why the conversation had been so reassuring.

The villagers were troubled to see Gar and Alea leave the next day and reminded them several times to beware of General Malachi. They did make sure the peddlers carried a good lunch with them, though.

They left a little after dawn, so they were several miles away when the bandit patrol found them in midmorning.

Gar heard their thoughts several miles away, of course, and told Alea, but didn't start fully cringing until they were only half a mile distant. She could hear their thoughts clearly and didn't like what she heard when they came in sight of her.

There were six of them, and the leader cried "Halt!" as he drew up in front of her. One of his men stopped beside him, but the other four went past her, two taking up station behind the pair, with one to either side.

"No seven-footer here, Sergeant," one of the men pointed out.

Gar stared up at him fearfully, then frowned, pointing from one horse-hoof to another and saying, "One . . . two . . . three . . . five . . . six . . . No!" He turned his finger back to the first horse and started over. "One . . . two . . . three . . . four . . . six . . . No! One . . . two . . . three . . . four . . . six . . . No . . ."

"What's the feeb doing?" the sergeant demanded irritably.

"Counting feet," Alea explained. "You said there was no seven-footer here. Please excuse my brother, Sergeant. His brain never grew much."

The other riders were grinning, but the sergeant looked disgusted. "Tell him he can stop—that we were looking for a man who's seven feet tall, not one who has seven feet." He looked Alea up and down and grinned slowly. "You're tall enough, though. Not seven feet maybe, but not far short either."

"I'm not a man," Alea said quickly.

"No, she sure ain't—is she, Sergeant?" the rider beside him asked, and the others chuckled.

"They don't see so many women," the sergeant explained. "You're a bit tall for my taste, but we got to take what we can get." He leaned down to hook a finger under her chin and lift; her skin crawled at his touch. "General Malachi says we can take what tolls we want from anyone on the roads."

7

Not from me you can't!" Alea swung her staff, knocking the sergeant's hand away.

"Well now, you shouldn'ta done that," the sergeant said, aggrieved, and sudden hands caught her shoulders and arms, yanking the staff out of her hand as the sergeant bent to seize her hair and drag her head back, laughing low in his throat as his broken-toothed grin came down over her lips.

It never touched. Gar erupted, roaring, yanking the sergeant off his horse and swinging him around in a circle, knocking the others away. He was a terrifying sight, eyes bulging, face swollen with rage, teeth flashing white in a space-tanned face, huge muscles rolling under naked skin as he threw the sergeant back across his horse and caught up Alea's staff to thrust it back into her hand, then crouched behind her, holding his staff like a baseball bat and bellowing, "Go! Leave sister 'lone!"

The sergeant pulled himself upright in his saddle, face white with fear—but as he felt his spear in his hand again, his courage came back and his look darkened. "Hold her, Arbin!" he snapped, then rode around to level his lance at Gar. "Ye don't strike Gin'ral Malachi's men, y'hear?"

Gar crouched cringing but roared defiance wordlessly—and clearly gathered himself to spring.

Even the sergeant took an involuntary step back, but he said, "Look around you, moron! There's four spears pointing at you and another three at your sister!"

"Not at sister!" Gar tensed, foam at his lips, the light of murder in his eyes.

"You didn't tell us that, now, did you?" The sergeant made it sound like a threat. "If we'd known she was your sister—well, we'd never trouble a sister where her brother had to watch, would we, boys?"

The bandits chorused doubtful nays, but Alea heard their thoughts and clamped her jaw against the bile that tried to rise in her gorge.

"We might stay to have some fun with you, though," the sergeant concluded.

Gar growled low in his throat, lifting the staff a little higher over his shoulder, and the light in his eyes turned to madness.

"Sergeant," one of the men said uncomfortably, "this ain't what we're sent to do."

"No, it ain't," the sergeant told Gar grimly, "and lucky for you that is, for we can't take the time to punish you now. But if you see the Gin'ral's soldiers again, you do what they tell you and do it quick, you hear?"

Gar's growl rose, his muscles bulging.

"I don't think he can understand so many words at once, Sergeant," Alea said quickly.

"Well then, you take your time and explain it to him, woman," the sergeant said with heavy emphasis. "It would be too bad if he went and skewered himself on our spears, it would."

Gar rose slightly from his crouch, the staff still high, the growl still in his throat.

"You're warned!" the sergeant said, and turned his horse. He trotted off down the road; his men followed, looking back with glances that were either lustful or fearful, then turning away to ride on behind the sergeant.

Alea watched them go, trembling with relief and fear—of them, the fear had to be of them, and as soon as they were out of sight she turned on Gar. "You interfering lummox! I was afraid I was going to see you turned into a pincushion! Didn't you realize you could be hurt?"

"I was more concerned about you," Gar said gravely.

Something melted inside Alea, but she coated it with steel and ranted on. "I would have survived—and you don't think I would have let them really do anything to me, do you? Believe me, every one of them would have paid dearly for what he did!"

"I don't doubt it," Gar replied, "but I would rather they didn't do it in the first place."

Alea ignored him. "Never mind that you straightened up! They must have seen how tall you are! By now they'll have realized you're the man they're hunting and be calling up a hundred more to bring you in!"

Gar gazed off into space a moment, his face going blank; Alea could have screamed until she realized he was listening for the patrol's thoughts. She tried it herself and caught a jumble of accusations and counteraccusations, of denials and insults; none of the men would admit having been afraid of the mad half-wit. All agreed he should be locked up, not allowed to wander the roads. None, however, volunteered to go back with a net and chains.

"It never even occurred to them," Gar told her. "I went from being a toad to a gorilla and back to a toad. None of them thought I might be the man and warrior for whom they're looking."

"They were ready to kill you on the spot!"

"None of them could admit they were afraid," Gar explained. "They had to threaten me enough to prove it, but they weren't really about to push the simpleton so hard that he might attack again."

Alea frowned. "How could they tell?"

"I didn't explode until they threatened you," Gar explained. "They knew 'poor Gar' wouldn't mind what they said about him, only about his sister—unless they actually attacked."

"You don't really think you drove them away, do you?"

"Not really, no," Gar said. "I only made them realize that the cost of their fun would be higher than they wanted to pay."

"But they might have stabbed you six ways at once! You could have left it to me! I could have talked them out of it without coming to blows—I've done it before!" But she remembered the terror she'd felt when the hands seized her from behind and wasn't so sure.

Gar frowned, studying her, then said, "I'm sure you could have. Very well, I'll try to be a little more circumspect in the future."

Alea eyed him narrowly. "What does *that* mean?"

"It means I'll give you a chance to talk them out of it," Gar said, "and if they won't talk, I'll use telekinesis to make them have accidents, such as two of their horses stumbling at the same time and throwing their riders into each other—coincidentally, of course."

"Of course," Alea said dryly. "Well, thank you for trusting me enough to let me try—and for trying to protect me this time."

"You helped me escape General Malachi's camp," Gar reminded. "You guard my back, I'll guard your back."

"That sounds like a good bargain," Alea said, relenting. "Just wait until I need it, all right?"

"All right," Gar agreed, and fell in beside her as she turned away to take up the journey again. She found his presence very reassuring, and felt a secret glow within her knowing that he had tried to protect her.

They were welcomed in the next town with the delight with which everyone greets a break in monotony. The trade was brisk; this village's specialty was exquisitely carved figurines of several different kinds of hardwood, and they were all eager for new pans, beads, needles, pins, and even some of the pottery from the village only a few miles away—Gar found that amusing, and Alea, raised in a hamlet herself, wondered why.

Again Gar and Alea were invited to spend the night with one of the village family; Gar was amazed that these people felt they could trust total strangers and thought that perhaps they really didn't know what theft and violence were.

Alea was concerned about one of the children who coughed all evening and found a chance to ask his mother Celia, too quietly for little Orgo to hear, "Is he ill?"

"Only a cold, pray the Goddess," Celia said, but her face was shadowed with concern. "He's had it for two weeks, though, and I think it's growing worse."

"Don't you have a doctor here, or a wise woman?"

"Only old Priscilla," Celia said. "She's told me to put hot compresses on his chest at night and have him breathe over a steaming bowl when his head feels too full. I should take him to the temple."

Alea was surprised to hear a temple mentioned instead of a

doctor but reminded herself that monks and nuns of many different faiths had been healers. "That might be well," she agreed.

In the middle of the night, a rasping and gargling woke her. She lifted her head, frowning and looking about—then saw Orgo, his face turning blue.

Celia reached the little boy a second before her. "What's happened, Orgo? Here, try to spit, then breathe!

Orgo opened his mouth and made a hacking sound, but nothing came out and no breath came in.

"My boy is dying!" Celia cried, beside herself. "Gorbo! Gorbo, call the priestess!"

The oldest boy, pale with fright, pulled on his trews and ran out the door. His father came over, wide-eyed with apprehension.

Alea pressed her lips thin in exasperation. Surely the consolations of religion were important, but wouldn't a doctor . . . Then she remembered that here, the priestess probably *was* the doctor.

The temple must be far away, though; she hadn't seen it in the village. She turned to Gar, who was levering himself up. *Do something!*

"Go find me a clean piece of hollow straw with thick walls," Gar told her. He knelt and laid his ear against the boy's chest, then thumped with his thumb. He looked up at the anxious parents. "Bartrum, Celia—I can save his life, but I'll have to make a small cut in his skin. Do you wish me to do it?"

They stared in shock. Then Celia said, "But . . . but you're a half-wit!"

"Bandits struck him on the head two years ago," Alea said quickly. "Since then, his wits come and go. Thank your gods that they have come back now."

Inside her mind, Gar's voice spoke with approval: *Good improvisation.*

"I thank the God indeed," Bartrum said fervently, and Celia cried, "Do what you have to! Only save him!"

"Hold him still, Bartrum," Gar said to the father, "and don't be frightened by what I do." To the mother, "Bring me the candle; I must heat the blade."

She brought the candle with a trembling hand. Gar held the blade in the flame; then Alea watched closely as he performed an emergency tracheotomy. Celia cried out in despair as she saw Orgo's blood—then wept with relief as she heard his breath whistle in.

The blueness faded from Orgo's face. His breath rasped, but he began to regain the ruddiness of health.

"His voicebox was clogged with the mucus from his chest," Gar explained to Celia and Bartrum. "He can't breathe forever through that straw, but it will keep him until your priestess can come."

"Thank the gods that you knew what to do," Bartrum said in a shaky voice.

"He won't have that thing there forever, will he?" Celia asked anxiously.

"No, but there will probably be a small scar."

"Little enough price for his life," Celia said. "Oh, thank you, Gar! The Mother-Goddess must have sent you here!"

Gar didn't answer, but Alea could see his face glow in the candlelight.

"Thank you, thank you a thousand times, Gar," Bartrum seized his hand and pumped it fervently.

Gar frowned vaguely, looking down at their joined hands, then back up at Bartrum's face, and the light of intelligence faded from his eyes. "Thank?" he asked. "Why?"

"For my son's life, of course!" Then Bartrum realized what was happening and dropped Gar's hand. "Oh . . . my friend . . ."

"Yes," Alea said softly. "His wits have fled again. It was only Orgo's dire need that brought them back, I guess."

"Or the Goddess." Celia stroked sweat from her child's brow. "Lie easy, son. The priestess will be here soon enough."

She was indeed; not even half an hour later, the priestess came in the door, face taut with urgency, and looked about her. "Where is the child? . . . Oh!"

"The strangers saved him," Celia told her.

The priestess came over to study the tracheotomy closely and frowned. "This was well done, but it will not endure. Still, it will hold till we have brought him to the temple." She called over her shoulder, "Take him up!"

Two brawny young men in leather jerkins and hose came into the house. They wore bows and quivers slung over their backs and thick knobbed sticks at their belts. They spread a stretcher next to Orgo and lifted him onto it.

"Lie still, my son." Celia stroked his brow. "They will carry you to the temple, and how many other boys can say they have had such a privilege?"

In spite of it all, Orgo's eyes lit with eagerness.

The priestess reached out a hand to the boy's throat. "This took skill and great knowledge." She turned to Alea. "You did well, lady."

"Oh, not I," Alea protested. "There sits your surgeon."

The priestess turned and stared at Gar.

The big man sat on his heels against the wall, rocking back and forth, staring at the coals on the hearth with a vacant face.

"How is this?" The priestess frowned. "Do you mean to tell me a simpleton could work such surgery?"

"He is more than he seems," Alea said quickly, "and perhaps less, too." She caught a wordless but indignant burst of thought from Gar and stifled a smile.

The priestess studied Gar, still frowning, and for a moment Alea was afraid she was reading *his* mind—but she turned to Celia and said, “There is some urgency still. Come if you wish.”

“I shall,” Celia said instantly, and turned to Bartrum. “Stay with the others, my dear!”

Bartrum could only nod, mute, and the priestess gestured to her escort. They lifted Orgo onto the stretcher and carried him out—but two more came in and stood to either side of Gar.

Alea looked up, tensed to fight.

The priestess said, “The one with the damaged mind must come, too.”

Gar only blinked around him, confused. One of the guards caught him by the arm and said, “Come along now, fellow. We’ve a nice soft bed for you, and good food.”

“Food?” Gar asked hopefully.

“Sweet food,” the guard confirmed, “good food. Come on, now.” He started toward the door and Gar came willingly. His thought spoke in Alea’s mind: *I’ll be back soon enough, I’m sure, Wait here.*

Hanged if I will! Alea hurried after him and said, “May I not come too, lady? He’s my brother, and I’m concerned for him!”

“Yes, of course, lass,” the priestess said with gentle sympathy. “Mind you, I’m not saying we can cure him.”

“I don’t want to be parted from him, that’s all—at least, not while he’s like this!”

“You’re a good woman to take care of him so,” the priestess assured her. “Come with us, then.”

Alea remembered her manners and turned back to say quickly, “Thank you, Bartrum and Celia. Your hospitality . . .”

Celia cut her off. “Hospitality! My child’s life! Thank *you*, Alea, and your brother! May the gods watch over you as you have watched over us!”

"My life is yours," Bartrum said fervently. "Anything I can give, you've but to ask."

"Come along, child," the priestess said with a touch of impatience.

"Good-bye, then," Alea said to her host, and hurried out the door beside her hostess.

The temple stood atop an oblong hill a mile outside of the village, all columns and pediments, gleaming silver in the moonlight. Across from it stood a second temple, similar but of a darker stone—it was impossible to tell its color in the moonlight.

From the summit, Alea could look down at half a dozen other sleeping villages and understood that the temples weren't located in any one because they had to serve all.

A boy god and a girl god . . . Alea remembered the child's statement of their religion and concluded that one temple must be for the god, the other for the goddess—but the priestess was going toward the silvered temple, Celia close behind, and Alea went with her.

They came up a broad flight of steps, then in among the columns, and Alea saw they were of marble, very pale. Great bronze doors decorated with sculptured motifs opened to them; they went through.

Alea stopped, awestruck by the huge statue of a woman with a strong but gentle face, simply robed, smiling with affection and welcome. In one arm she held a cornucopia, in the other a bow.

"Why, child," said the priestess, "have you never seen a statue of the goddess?"

"Never . . . never quite like this." Indeed, the statue seemed very much like Freya but also very much like Idun. There was something of the Valkyrie about her, too. It was as though all the Germanic goddesses had been blended into one.

She forced herself to turn away and was surprised to discover that she automatically spoke in a hush. "You cannot work cures in a place of reverence such as this."

"No. That we must do below." The priestess gestured toward her right.

Looking, Alea saw the guards disappearing down a broad stairway, Celia right behind them. With a little cry, Alea started after.

"Gently, child, gently." The priestess touched her shoulder.

Looking back, Alea saw that she smiled with kindly amusement.

"Your brother will wait for us," the priestess assured her. "First, though, it is you who must wait for him."

She led Alea to an anteroom where there were padded chairs with small tables between. Pastel frescoes brightened the walls.

"Bide here in patience," the priestess said. "An acolyte will bring you refreshment. Your brother will be with you in an hour or so. Then we shall tell you if we can do anything to heal his brain."

"Heal his brain?" Alea started up in alarm. "What do you mean to do?"

"Now, now, we only mean to discover the cause of his wits coming and going," the priestess said in a soothing tone. "We will not truly do anything to him without telling you and having your consent."

Alea sat back but eyed the priestess warily.

"Trust the goddess, my dear," the priestess said with a reassuring touch on her hand, then turned through the curtained archway and was gone.

Alea sat alone, frowning at the murals and trying to puzzle out the story from what was shown there. She saw a young man in rough garb gazing through the rushes at the side of a pond;

within the water stood a young woman, and the positions of her hands showed that she was bathing, but her body was only a burst of brightness, and the expression on the young man's face was awe. The young woman, however, seemed irritated, as any young woman might be in her place. Nearby, six hounds lay; two were coming to their feet.

Footsteps padded, and Alea looked up to see a sleepy teenage girl bearing a tray with some small cakes, a tall pitcher, and a cup. She set them on the little table beside Alea, then stepped back, saying, "Do you need anything more, Lady?"

"No . . . no, this will do well." Alea smiled at the younger woman. "I thank you—and I am sorry to disturb your sleep."

The girl smiled in return. "We who would serve the goddess must be ever ready to come to her service, Lady. Do not hesitate to call out if you have need."

"Thank you," Alea said. "I shall."

"I saw you studying the picture." The girl turned to gaze at the mural, too. "It would seem to be only the huntsman coming upon the goddess unadorned, in her role as maiden and hunter, for which offense, unintended or not, he died—but the priestesses tell me there is a deeper meaning hidden in the story, even a Mystery." She turned back to Alea with a smile of embarrassment. "I have not yet discovered it, though. I have a great deal to learn."

"So have I," Alea said, "but since I must wait here, I shall contemplate the scene. Perhaps I shall discover what it represents."

"Perhaps so. I wish you good fortune." But the girl's eyes went round in awe and she made a small curtsy before she went out again.

Alea frowned after her, wondering what had bothered the girl—then realized that the lass thought Alea must needs be an initiate to be able to speak of discovering a Mystery.

Well, perhaps she would at that, though not in the way the acolyte thought. Alea composed herself, gazing at the mural as though in meditation—but as her body relaxed and stilled, her mind opened, seeking the thoughts of the people within this temple—first Orgo, who was still in peril despite Gar's temporary surgery, then Gar himself.

If she could still find him.

8

Orgo was underneath the temple asleep; Alea wondered how he could nod off in the midst of such turmoil, then realized the two who bore him must have given him a sleeping draft—for she was surprised to discover that their minds were not those of the guards; the priestess's escort must have handed the boy over to these two priests as soon as they had carried the boy to the stairwell.

The priests—scarcely more than acolytes, she realized from their talk—were standing in a small room beside Orgo's stretcher, chatting about the "case," as they called the boy. There was a slight jarring and the doors of the room slid back. The men carried the stretcher—no, it was a sort of table with wheels; they must have put Orgo on it when the guards brought the boy to them. They rolled him into a large room and lifted him onto a bed with a sort of tunnel over it. They pushed the bed into the tunnel, then watched a set of pictures on its side—and wonder of wonders, Alea could see inside Orgo! One picture showed his bones, and the flesh seemed ghostly over them; another showed his lungs, but they weren't light and empty, as she always had thought lungs should be; they seemed cloudy, with only the very top being completely clear.

"Congested," one of the young priests said, "and he's picked up some kind of a germ that caused an overabundance of mucus."

"An antibiotic should take care of it."

Alea listened to them discuss whether or not they would need a surgeon, blood chilled; she knew that a surgeon meant cutting—but the young priests decided that they could wait a day or two and see what the drugs would do. Alea didn't understand all their words, but she caught the gist—that they were going to give Orgo some sort of medicine, and that he would live.

But what a wondrous assortment of machinery they had! She was sure it was machinery—she had seen enough of Herkimer to know that, and seen the pictures of modern civilizations he had shown her. What were such wonders doing here in a Neolithic society?

Time later to consider the question—first she had to find Gar. She opened her mind wide again, expanding her attention to include the whole temple and the hill on which it stood until she recognized the overtones of his thoughts. She narrowed her attention to include only Gar and the priest and priestess who spoke to him.

He was far underground, too, in a small room that was painted in earth tones with lovely pictures stirring on the walls—amazingly, the trees and flowers they showed moved in an unseen breeze. Gar sat in a padded chair, one with a back high enough to cushion even his head. The priest and priestess sat in similar chairs, the priest behind a desk with a screen inset; from time to time, he glanced at the screen to make sure the transcription of their interview was proceeding properly. It was; words rolled up across the screen in even lines.

The colonists had buried their spaceship, Alea realized, or perhaps only one of their landing craft—she suspected there were many hills like this throughout the land. The ancestors must have come in a fleet and left their descendants the machinery and chemicals of modern medicine. What had Gar said—that the colonists had cheated? He would certainly think so now!

"Good, then." The priestess smiled, relaxing. "You see, we *are* your friends."

Alea wondered how she had gone about proving that and how long Gar had pretended to remain suspicious, simply to be believable. On the other hand, perhaps he hadn't been pretending. Somehow she doubted that they had his full confidence even now.

"Friends." Gar smiled, nodding eagerly.

"Can you remember someone striking you on the head?" the priestess asked.

Gar screwed up his face, rolling up his eyes with the effort of concentration, then shook his head.

"Total amnesia, then," the priest said.

The priestess nodded, still looking at Gar. "Can you remember going to sleep tonight?"

Gar nodded like a puppy wanting to please.

"Do you remember trading with the villagers?"

Again, Gar screwed up his face in concentration. After a minute, he nodded, but with much less certainty.

"Do you remember waking up yesterday morning?"

Again the screwed up face, but this time, Gar shook his head sadly.

"Quite a bit of damage indeed." The priestess slipped the chain that held her medallion over her head and held it out, the glittering medal swinging like a pendulum. "Is not my jewelry pretty?"

"Pretty," Gar agreed, his eyes glued to the silvery object. He braced himself to resist hypnosis.

"Follow it with your eyes." The priestess moved it to her right; Gar's eyes followed. "Now the other way." The bauble moved to the left; still Gar's eyes followed. "Up . . . down . . . He has no difficulty tracking."

"We can hope it is only his recall that is impaired," the priest said. "Given time, the brain should find a way to access the memories from another site."

"Let us see if we can hasten the process." The priestess twitched her fingers and the medallion began to swing like a pendulum again. "Watch the medallion, Gar . . . see how it swings . . . to the left . . . to the right . . ."

Gar followed the pendulum intently, even turning his head a little.

Alea thought he was overdoing it.

The priest yawned, and the priestess said, "How very late it is . . . I am so sleepy . . . It would be sweet to sleep . . . sleep . . . you are sleepy too, Gar . . . so sleepy . . . your eyelids are so heavy you can scarcely keep them open . . . sleep . . . sleep . . ." She lowered the medallion.

Gar kept his head turning from side to side.

The priestess smiled. "You may hold your head still, Gar."

Gar gazed straight forward, letting his eyes lose focus.

"What is your name?" the priestess asked.

"Gar," he said, like a sleepwalker.

"What is your last name?"

"Last . . . ?" Gar risked a little frown even though he was supposed to be entranced.

Alea sighed with relief. The hypnotism hadn't worked, but he was quick to pretend it had.

"No last name," the priest said. "Only a peasant, it would seem."

"Who gave you your name, Gar?"

"Priest," Gar muttered thickly.

"A priest? Good, that's progress. . . . Who told the priest what name to give?"

"Mama," Gar said. "Papa . . ."

"What did your mother look like, Gar?"

"Big," Gar said. "Huge, like tree. Red hair, green eyes . . . smile . . ."

"He's seeing her as a baby would," the priest said.

"That's very good," the priestess said to both him and Gar. "You're a little older now . . . you're six . . . do you have a brother?"

Gar nodded.

"What's his name?"

"Geoffrey," Gar said, "and the baby."

Alea wondered if that was true or if Gar was making it up. He had never mentioned a brother. With a start, she realized he had never mentioned his family at all. She really didn't know a great deal about him, did she?

She felt a little angry about it. That would have to be remedied!

"Geoffrey is the baby?" the priestess asked.

Gar shook his head.

"What's the baby's name?"

"Gregory." Gar's voice had deepened and his words weren't slurring as badly.

Alea still thought he was overdoing it. Would a brain-damaged man recover himself that quickly?

"Very good," said the priestess. "Did you have a sister, too?"

Gar nodded.

"That would be Alea, of course," the priestess said. "Do you have only the one sister?"

"Only the one," Gar's voice was quite clear now. "I felt sorry for Mother sometimes."

"Vocabulary improved," the priest said, surprised. "He seems to have acquired a cultured accent."

"Yes, but not one I have ever heard." The priestess frowned. "Where is your home, Gar?"

"Gone from me." Gar's face crumpled. "Not in this world."

"Trauma," the priest whispered. "The bandits must have annihilated his whole village."

Well, that was one way to look at it, Alea decided, though it might have been more accurate to say Gar had gone from his home, not the other way around. Still, Gar hadn't actually lied. Could he help it if they misinterpreted the strict truth?

Of course he could, she thought, but admitted that under the circumstances, misleading them was probably the wiser course.

"He seems to have accessed another area of memory," the priest said, "and bypassed the damaged area."

The priestess nodded. "I thought he must be capable of something like that, since his sister said his memory comes and goes."

Ingenious improvisation, Alea, Gar thought. *You're very quick.*

Alea started. How had Gar known she was listening in? But come to think of it, what else would she be doing?

"Now, Gar." The priestess tensed, frowning. "Where did you learn medicine?"

Even with so much rock and metal between them, Alea could feel her anxiety and that of her priest-companion. Their alarm was clear: that anyone but a priest or priestess should have advanced scientific knowledge.

"Medicine . . . ?" Gar's face was blank.

The priestess studied him for a moment and Alea could feel her massive relief in the thought: *He knows nothing about medicine, then.* She tried another approach. "The operation you did for little Orgo. Where did you learn to perform a tracheotomy?"

"Surgery." Gar's face cleared. "I had to help a wise woman once—emergency, like Orgo's. I held the man still with his arms to his sides and watched closely while she made the cut; I knew I might need it to save a life someday."

"Only by watching?" the priestess pressed. "No one ever taught you to do it?"

Gar turned his head from side to side. "Only watched." Then, anxiously, "Did I do it correctly?"

Priest and priestess both relaxed. The priestess smiled as she said, "Yes, Gar, you did it well—very well indeed; you saved Orgo's life." Then, to the priest, "He must be very intelligent when his mind is awake."

"Very good memory, too," the priest agreed.

"All right, now, Gar," the priestess said, "I'm going to wake you up." She coached him back to the present, brought him to a very light trance, then said, "When I clap my hands you'll be completely awake, but you won't remember anything of what we've said. Is that clear?"

"Clear," Gar muttered.

The priestess clapped her hands; Gar blinked, then looked around him as though wondering how he'd come to be there.

"Surely you remember coming down here with us," the priest cajoled.

"Coming . . . down here?" Gar frowned intently, then nodded. " 'Member."

"He's lost his memory again." The priestess sighed. "I had hoped he could hold on to it once the link was established."

"No doubt it will reestablish itself more often," the priest told her.

"Yes, we'll have done that much good, at least. Well, Gar, would you like some breakfast now?"

Half an hour later, Alea led her "brother" down the hillside. When they were several hundred yards from the temples, Alea said, "Well, you certainly had your chance to learn about the religion here. Anything interesting?"

"The underground chambers, for one," Gar said. "Metal walls and plastic chairs aren't exactly Neolithic, let alone sliding doors. Their ancestors became mound builders, covering the landing craft with dirt and calling them hills, then building the temples on top."

Alea nodded. "Did you read the minds of the priest and priestess who were taking care of Orgo?"

"No, I was a little preoccupied," Gar confessed. "What did they do?"

"Took him deep underground to a room where there was one of those X-ray machines Herkimer told me about," Alea said, "though maybe it was a sonograph or a CAT scanner."

"Something that let them look inside the boy, anyway."

Alea nodded. "They found his throat was clogged with mucus and said they'd give him one of those pills you told me about, the kind that kill germs. You know, I hadn't thought germs were real, just something Herkimer made up, but those priests couldn't have talked with him."

"No, though I wouldn't be surprised if they had a computer with a database like his," Gar said, "just a much older version." He smiled. "Well, it may not be terribly Neolithic, but it does fit the priestly role of healer."

"Yes, it does." When she'd learned they were going to visit a Neolithic society, Alea had studied everything about them that Herkimer had on file. "That's why the temple isn't in the village—each ship has to care for a whole district."

"But the original colonists had a problem," Gar said. "They wanted to make modern medicine available to their descendants, but they didn't want to contaminate their brand-new Neolithic civilization with modern machinery and the industrial civilization that would go with it."

"So they passed the knowledge down through the clergy," Alea said. "I'll bet they don't teach the priests and priestesses about the machines until they've taken their final vows and committed themselves completely to the temples."

"And one of those vows is an oath not to talk about anything modern with anybody who isn't a priest." Gar smiled, amused. "No wonder they went into a panic when I performed a tracheotomy!"

"Well, I wouldn't call it a panic," Alea demurred. "I do think they're aware that this knowledge gives them power and status, though. They don't want to lose that, so they're very worried if someone else has their knowledge."

"Especially if that someone is a common peasant," Gar said with a sardonic smile. "Still, I think they're at least as worried about protecting their society from the modern world as they are about keeping their position. I wonder how their ancestors managed to pass on their fear of contamination?"

"Probably through stories," Alea said. "I'd love to hear their myths." She remembered how she and Gar had made up tales that were even now helping change her home world.

"Good thought." Gar nodded. "I wonder how many other advanced techniques the clergy are using, disguised as religious rituals."

Alea frowned. "Why would there be any need for anything but healing to be modern?"

"Because with advanced medical services," Gar said, "people live longer, and the population grows—especially when women live until menopause and after; they can bear more children."

Alea frowned. "Who says they have to?"

"Their societies, usually," Gar said, "even their religions—or they did, in the Neolithic era. With short life spans and a lot of babies dying at birth or soon after, they needed to keep the birth rate up so the tribe wouldn't die off. We don't have any evidence that they thought about birth control—but these people must, or there would be too many of them and not enough food."

"More people makes for more hands to do the work," Alea argued. "They could have all the babies they want if they grow more food!"

"Not enough more," Gar said, "unless they used modern farming techniques like crop rotation and spreading fertilizer. I'll bet you the priests and priestesses do both under the guise of ritual."

Alea eyed him warily. "What's the stake?"

For a moment, Gar's eyes gleamed with admiration and desire; then the look was gone, hidden under the mask of his constant courtesy, leaving Alea shaken, relieved, and disappointed all at the same time. She gathered anger to hide her confusion. "Never mind. I don't know if I want to gamble with you of all people."

"I'm not usually a betting man," Gar told her, "and I meant it more as a figure of speech than a serious wager. Still, I'll settle for the loser admitting the winner was right."

Alea's anger focused into indignation that he would even ask such a lessening of her pride—but she remembered it might be he who applauded her good sense. "I'll take that bet." She wondered what stakes had been his first impulse—a kiss, or more?—and felt a wave of regret that he had bitten back the words. Still, that regret was mingled with relief, but also amazement that he had shown some feeling for her other than friendship and admiration.

Well, little good would it do him, and if he ate his heart out watching her, so much the better! She lifted her chin and said, "You don't fool me. You're hoping the priests and priestesses will turn out to be a government dressed in ceremonial robes."

"A theocracy? Yes, the thought had occurred to me," Gar confessed. "It wouldn't be the first time a church has taken up the functions of a government when there was none." He looked up at the sky. "There isn't all that much of the night left, but I confess I'd like to sleep while I can. Shall we go back to Bartrum and Celia's cottage?"

Bartrum was waiting up nervously and was massively relieved to hear that Orgo was well and would be as good as new, but that he would have to stay at the temple for a day or two until the priestess was sure the illness had run its course. He cobbled up a late supper; then everyone went back to sleep again.

They all woke late, by farm standards—it must have been an hour past sunrise at least—and ate a leisurely breakfast with their host. Celia arrived home while they were eating, worn but happy. Bartrum fussed over her, making sure she joined them to eat, and wouldn't leave off until he was sure she felt somewhat restored. Then he turned to Gar and Alea with an apologetic smile and explained, "My friends won't blame me if I come late to the plowing this morning."

"Is it your turn to work in the fields, then?" Gar asked.

Bartrum glanced at Celia; she shrugged and said, "Bartrum

doesn't mind the plowing much. I hate it. I go for the sowing, though."

"We do take turns during hoeing season," Bartrum told them, "and of course we both go to the reaping—all of us, in fact."

"So it's up to each family," Gar summarized.

"Of course." Bartrum frowned. "Isn't that how they do it in your country, friend?"

"More or less," Gar said. "I've never really thought of it much."

Alea gave him a quick glance. Never before had she heard him say anything about his station in life on his home world—not that she could trust what he was saying when he was trying to draw out his hosts, of course.

"It's just something we all do," Gar said, "just the way it's done."

Bartrum nodded; he could understand the dictates of custom. "Among us, each couple decides for themselves," he said. "No one minds so long as each household does its share of the work."

Gar didn't have to ask what happened if they didn't. He knew what social pressure was—that didn't take a government.

When they were about to leave on the northern road, Bartrum warned them, "Go warily. We've been hearing more reports of outlaws these last few months."

"Outlaws, not just bandits?" Gar turned to him, fairly glowing with interest.

"Well, of course they're both," Celia said, puzzled at his eagerness.

"I haven't heard any talk of laws here," Gar said. "What are they?"

"Oh, the laws everyone knows," Bartrum said. "You must

respect your elders, mustn't start a fight, mustn't steal or lie or cheat."

"You shouldn't want more than you need," Celia added, "and you mustn't try to make other people do things they don't want to do—and of course, you should honor the gods."

"As many as that?" Gar asked, wide-eyed. Only Alea could hear the irony in his tone and perhaps even she only detected it because she was picking up his emotions.

"Only that," Celia concurred, "but simply because *we* know the laws doesn't mean the outlaws honor them. Be careful, friends!"

"Be careful," Bartrum seconded, "and remember that if you ever need anything, you have only to ask it of your friends here."

Alea hugged Celia impulsively while Gar clasped Bartrum's hand. "Thank you for this timely warning." He turned to Alea. "Perhaps we should stay awhile; profit does us little good if it's stolen."

Alea understood that the remark was only a show for their hosts' benefit. "How else would we live? Or are you ready to settle down and farm?"

Gar glanced out at the fields and Alea was startled to see a sort of hunger in his eyes—but he said slowly, "No, not yet."

"Then we had best be on our way," Alea said briskly, and hugged Celia again. "Thank you ever so much for your hospitality!"

"Thank you ever so much for my son's life," Celia returned. "Oh, take care, my friends! Take care!"

When they were too far away for the couple to hear, though they were still waving good-bye, Gar said, "We shall certainly take care—unlike General Malachi, who will take everything he can!"

"At least they've had the good sense to declare him an outlaw," Alea said.

"That is hopeful," Gar agreed, "and common law is better than none. Interesting to see that they've developed eight of the Ten Commandments and a variation on the Golden Rule."

"Ten Commandments? What are those?" Alea asked, frowning, and when Gar explained, she admitted, "My people only had seven of those but quite a few others besides. Still, those seven must be so vital that no nation could last without them!"

"I shouldn't think so," Gar agreed. "After all, if you don't have a law forbidding murder, what's to keep your people from killing each other off?"

Alea shuddered but said bravely, "And if you don't insist that it's wrong to steal, neighbors can't trust one another."

Gar nodded. "Strange that they don't have a law against incest, though. If people marry their first cousins for too many generations, the whole society falls apart from madness and idiocy."

Alea glanced at him sharply "How do you know that?"

Gar shrugged. "The only societies that are alive and well are the ones that prohibit inbreeding. Any that ever permitted it have died off as I've said."

"So your evidence is that there isn't any evidence?"

"No, a bit more than that," Gar said slowly. "There have been quite a few royal families that insisted on brothers marrying sisters and first cousins marrying first cousins so that the magical royal blood would be kept within the family and not contaminated by commoners—until the last kings were so weak and stupid that they became easy prey to ambitious outsiders."

"That makes sense." Alea frowned. "My . . . Midgard's laws forbid murder, incest, and theft, but of course they don't apply to slaves, or to dwarves or giants."

"Of course not," Gar said. "In Neolithic societies, the laws usually apply only within your own group. It's perfectly all right to go stealing from that tribe over the hill—in fact, it's a virtue, if you don't get caught."

Alea smiled bleakly; thinking of her homeland saddened and angered her, as it always did. "My people do insist on honoring the gods, though, or at least paying them lip service."

"A Neolithic god is a model for living," Gar agreed. "You try to be as much like the god of your choice as you can, live the way he or she lived."

Alea smiled sourly. "If that's the case, General Malachi should be inventing a god of thieves and a god of warriors."

"Why not?" Gar shrugged. "Other Neolithic societies did."

If General Malachi had invented a thieves' god he must have been praying to his homemade deity, because Gar and Alea encountered his soldiers again in midmorning. They were approaching a stand of trees where the road made a bend.

"Men talking on the other side of that curve," Gar said. "They're taking a rest from riding. They could be ordinary plowmen, or they could be one of Malachi's patrols."

"Let's not take chances," Alea said. "Into the trees."

"Forests are friendly," Gar agreed, and they stepped off the road, pushed their way through underbrush, and came into the green and leafy spaces. They moved through the woods carefully, making very little noise, cutting across the bend to come up behind the men. They could hear their loud talk and raucous laughter a hundred yards away and stopped at fifty feet, peering through the screen of brush to see whether or not the men wore General Malachi's uniform.

"Whatcha lookin' at, half-wit?" snarled a gravelly voice, and a boot caught Gar on the side, tumbling him over with a startled cry.

9

Alea spun in alarm, trying to strike with her staff, but she didn't have room for a proper swing and the man caught the stick in one hand while he caught her wrist in the other. Grinning, he said, "Don't just watch, sweetheart," and shoved his face forward for a kiss.

His breath reeked. Revolted, Alea kicked as hard as she could. The man yelped and let go to catch at his shin, hopping about.

"Ho, Arbaw! Hold her!"

Alea looked up in alarm. The soldiers from the roadside were running toward them, weaving in and out among the trunks. She blessed the trees for slowing them down even as she turned and ran.

But Arbaw snarled and caught her arm as she went past. She kicked at his other shin, but he managed to put the injured foot down in time to sidestep—and his weakened leg almost folded. Alea helped it, chopping her heel into the back of his knee. Arbaw howled and fell, but he dragged her with him.

He had delayed her long enough. The other bandit-soldiers burst from the trees with howls of glee. “Well caught, Arbaw!” one called. “Answer a call of nature, and see how Nature answers!”

Gar roared as he surged up charging. He slammed into one soldier, knocking him into another, then both into a third. But the remaining two men swerved and fell on him with bellows of outrage, pulling daggers from their belts. Gar shook off his attackers and spun away from the fallen men to kick and punch with a most un-idiotic skill and grace. One soldier fell back clutching his stomach, mouth open to gasp; the other flew through the air, and so did his dagger.

It landed three feet from Alea. She plunged, snatched it up, and turned to find Arbaw’s blade hovering inches in front of her eyes. “Put it down, sweetmeat,” he grunted, “or I’ll give you another mouth.”

Alea twisted to the side as she kicked him in the sweetbreads. Arbaw rolled away, clutching at himself and howling. Alea rolled the other way, pushed herself to her feet, caught up her staff, and swung it at the back of the head of one of Gar’s attackers. It cracked against his skull and the man fell. There were still two more worrying Gar like rats on a terrier; she jabbed one in the stomach with the butt of her staff. He folded as Gar slammed a huge fist into the other’s face.

“Run!” Alea shouted, and turned to flee through the woods. She heard feet pounding right behind her and looked back in a panic, but it was only Gar.

Finally they slowed and stopped, leaning against trees and gasping. “They’re not . . . following . . .” Gar wheezed.

“How come . . . you missed . . . Arbaw?” Alea asked.

“Sloppy,” Gar said with a grimace of self-disgust. “Very sloppy. I was . . . too intent on . . . the others.”

Alea could understand that; she had missed Arbaw, too, though she had the excuse of being a novice mind reader.

She finished catching her breath and straightened. "Two patrols is too many."

"You're right." Gar nodded. "Scaring the daylights out of one and beating up the other means they're going to remember us."

"And be looking for us," Alea agreed.

"No—me," he corrected. "They didn't get close enough to realize how tall you were, but both patrols will remember the half-naked idiot who turned into an ogre. They'll be looking for that idiot. If I change disguises, they won't recognize either of us."

"Well, I like that!" Alea said indignantly. "So I'm not worth noticing, am I?"

He stared at her, his gaze warming with admiration. "No man who's alive and healthy could keep from noticing you—but saying that a woman is beautiful isn't enough of a description for a patrol to recognize."

"But they'll recognize you, is that it? Because you're the important one?"

"No, because I'm the obvious one," Gar explained.

Alea reddened with increasing anger and snapped, "Are you really being as conceited as you sound?"

"Not a bit," Gar assured her. "People remember ugliness more than beauty!"

"You're not ugly!"

"Why, thank you," Gar said softly, "though I suspect you're the only one who would think so."

This wasn't going the way Alea wanted. "And I'm not beautiful."

"You're entitled to your own opinion," Gar said politely. "I'm afraid I don't share it, though."

"All right, *you* might notice me—but what other man would?"

"Too many, if the patrols we've found are anything to go by."

"Only because they're starved for women! The villagers only see me as a storyteller."

"How do you know," Gar asked, "when they're all noticing you?"

"You know very well how! A woman can tell the difference!"

"But she won't listen," Gar returned.

Alea's lips thinned. "They can all see I'm too tall for them, way too tall! And *that's* what the patrols will remember!"

"Not when they see you beside me," Gar said. "They can only judge our heights by each other, after all, and when they see you coming down the road with me cringing beside you, they assume you're of normal size."

"Until they get close!"

"When they come that close, they're more interested in making fun of the idiot."

Alea stared, catching her breath, then said, "You really are an arrogant cuss, aren't you?"

"It might seem that way," Gar admitted, "but it's really only camouflage."

"Camo-*what?*"

"Camouflage," Gar repeated, "fading into the background. Camouflage and misdirection, like songbirds."

Alea stared, completely lost. She took a breath and said, in as reasonable a tone as she could manage, "Gar—what are you talking about?"

"It's like birds," Gar explained. "The male has bright colors so that the cats will attack him and not notice the female."

Alea lifted her head slowly, bridling. "Surely—because males don't really matter!"

"That's right, because males can't lay eggs or bear offspring,"

Gar said with a sardonic smile. "As far as evolution is concerned, we're more expendable than you."

"So that's why you adopted such an odd disguise, is it?"

"One of the reasons," Gar admitted, "but I think it's time to change. I'm going to age remarkably, Alea."

"Do you really think that will make a difference?" Alea snapped.

"Wait and see," Gar told her. "Then you judge."

The man was old and stooped, back bent under the weight of his pack, leaning heavily on his staff as he hobbled along the road. His snowy beard was long, his hair a white fringe around the felt cap that fitted his head like a helmet—but his rough-hewn face really didn't have all that many wrinkles. His limbs were probably gnarled and wasted, but no one could tell under the long dark blue robe he wore.

The woman who held his arm was a complete contrast, straight and tall, glowing with youth and health, her head a little higher than his.

The farmers looked up as they passed, saw the packs, and cried, "Peddlers!" The shout passed from one to another all across the fields. They came running with their hoes and mattocks, crying,

"Welcome, travelers!"

"What wares have you to trade?"

"What news have you? What happens in the wide world?"

The next morning, they left the village with cheery good-byes and waving hands—and several beautifully wrought little items of gold and silver in their packs. As they turned to the road ahead, Alea said, "I can see that being a peddler in this land could be very profitable, even if they don't have money."

"We haven't had to pay for dinner or lodgings once," Gar agreed, "but we're not much richer in information than when we began. I still haven't heard anything about a government."

"And every time we bring up the subject of banditry, all we hear about is General Malachi," Alea sighed, "but never anything we don't already know."

"If he were as successful as his reputation," Gar grumbled, "he would already be king!"

"He'd rule this whole world," Alea agreed, "but is he really that bad, or is there just so little else to talk about?"

As they were leaving one village that lay within sight of the trees of a forest, though, the villagers were a bit more direct.

"Don't go through that woodland by yourselves," one woman warned them. "Wait for a larger party if you've an ounce of sense."

"Sense?" Gar asked in his rusty approximation of an old man's voice. He glanced up at Alea and asked again, "Sense?"

"I know, old fellow," a man sympathized, "if you had any sense, you wouldn't be walking the roads at your time of life anyway. But we have to make a living, don't we?" He transferred his gaze to Alea. "You might think of settling down someplace, lass, so that he can rest in his old age."

"I will if I find a town that wants me, and if I can persuade him to stay in one place for more than a week," Alea said, smiling.

"Till then, though, you'll have to do the thinking for your father." A woman blinked tears away. "Oh, do be wise and wait for other travelers!"

"That could be a month or more," Alea answered. "What can they take from us if we have nothing to steal?"

"Nothing but your bodies and your lives," the villager said darkly.

"You would be forced to serve General Malachi's bandits."

The woman shuddered. "Beware of that man, sister! If ever there was an ogre from out of the old tales, it is he!"

The patrols were still on the roads, but Gar heard their thoughts before they came into sight, giving himself and Alea time to hide—and they didn't try to spy on the soldiers as they went past any more, but concentrated on the soldiers not spying them.

Their welcome in the next village was as joyous as ever, but Gar decided to be a smart old man instead of a foolish one and drove bargains with every bit as much zeal as Alea. They traded the porcelains of their first village for uncut gemstones, though they had to add a few wedges of copper to make their hosts happy.

Once again Gar noticed people putting bits of metal in a collection box. This time, though, he was sure another one had put in a chip of something white.

Alea settled down to tell a story to the village children and their parents naturally stayed, too—only to keep an eye on their little ones, of course.

"Once upon a time, long ago and far away, there lived a man whose wife had died, leaving him with only one daughter . . ."

Murmurs of sympathy.

"After a few years, the man married again . . ."

"What is 'married'? " a young man asked.

Taken aback, Alea explained, "They lived together and reared a family."

"Oh, bonding." The man nodded; everyone else did, too, understanding. " 'Married . . .' an odd word. How many children did the new wife have?"

"Two daughters."

"The poor woman—only two. She must have loved having a third."

"Well, she seemed to, until her husband died," Alea said. "Then she made her stepdaughter do all the cooking and sweeping and scrubbing, and throwing out the garbage and tending the kitchen garden, while her own two girls slept as late as they wanted and spent the day amusing themselves."

She hadn't been prepared for the loud and instant protest, and the adults were almost as vociferous as the children.

"Her own daughters? They were all three her own daughters!" a woman said indignantly.

"And doubly precious if her husband had died," said an older woman who looked as though she knew.

"She really made the poor lass do all the housekeeping?" one mother asked indignantly. "Well, I never!"

"And all the cooking, too," another woman said, shaking her head with a dark frown. "Shameful, I call it."

But both of them were glancing out of the corners of their eyes at another older woman who reddened with anger but stood her ground, tilting up her chin. Gar wondered which child she favored.

"Now, in that country, there lived a . . ." Alea paused, remembering what had happened the last time she had referred to a king. ". . . a duke whose son was twenty-five and hadn't married yet. . . ."

"What's a duke?" one of the children piped up.

The parents nodded, equally puzzled.

"It's . . . um . . . a man who owns the land that the people of a hundred villages farm," Alea said, with a sinking feeling that already this was not going well. "He tells them all what work to do, and when." There, that didn't sound quite so bad as ordering them about.

It was bad enough.

"The very idea!" one woman said indignantly.

"That one man could dare to tell the people of a hundred villages what to do and not do!" a man said, equally indignant.

"Or even a dozen villages," another man chimed in.

"What a villain!" a second woman said.

"Well, every good tale must have a villain, must it not?" Alea tried not to look as nervous as she felt.

That silenced them for a minute. Brows bent, faces frowned while they mulled it over, darting dark suspicious glances at Gar and Alea. Then an old woman pronounced, "No. I know tales about folk braving natural hazards, such as clashing rocks and arid deserts—or monsters such as one-eyed giants, or manticores with a thousand shark teeth and stingers in their tails."

"Then think of a duke as a monster," Alea said, and inspiration struck. "Think of him as a bully who lords it over other bullies."

Their faces cleared; that, they could understand.

"Like this General Malachi we've heard of?" the first woman asked.

"The very thing!" Alea said with relief. "He's nothing but a bully who has herded a bunch of bandits together and made them fight for him."

The villagers looked around nervously, but nodded with energy.

Alea decided it was time to get back to the story. "Let's forget that the father was a duke—just think of him as a very rich man."

The villagers turned to one another in consternation, exchanging questions and a lack of answers.

Alea reined in exasperation and explained, "A rich man is one who has a great deal of . . ." No, they didn't seem to use money here. ". . . a great number of possessions."

"You mean he was the son of a priest?" a woman asked.

"Well . . . he lived with his family in a great house and wore beautiful clothes," Alea temporized, "and never had to plow or hoe."

"A priest indeed," the woman said, satisfied, and everyone else nodded, chorusing agreement.

"But he did learn to reap, of course," a man said.

"Of course," Alea said, a little unnerved. "Doesn't everybody?"

They all nodded, agreeing with that.

"Anyway," Alea said, "the priest decided that his son was old enough to mar . . . uh, to bond with a woman, past old enough, really, and told him that he must see to finding a wife, and sent messengers throughout the district for all the maidens to come to a grand feast he would give, so that his son might choose among them."

"Why would he do that?" one of the men asked, frowning.

"Aye!" said the woman by his side. "It's no good trying to find the right mate—these things simply happen."

"Or fail to," grunted one older man. He was rather ugly, and the woman's tone softened.

"Aye, some of us must wait longer than others, Holdar. But love comes to all someday."

"And it's worth the waiting for," said another man with a warm glance at the woman by his side. She returned the look, beaming, and took his hand.

"Um . . . Well, it may have been silly, but there are always people who have to prove for themselves what everybody knows," Alea said.

"Well, that's so, I suppose," a man allowed, and the neighbors set up another chorus of agreement.

Alea relaxed again, but not much, as she explained, "The son had been a bit wild, you see, and the priest wanted him tied to one woman, to settle him down."

"He *what?*" a man cried, aghast.

"You don't mean a *priest* would want a boy bonded to a girl for life!" a woman gasped.

"They might have fallen out of love!" another woman protested. "This priest wouldn't have them tied together when they didn't love one another, would he?"

Alea was stunned—here were ordinary villagers, most of them living as husband and wife with families, and they were frankly shocked at the idea of a man and woman bonding to live together for life.

"Everyone knows that's courting disaster," one woman declared.

That gave Alea gave back her poise. She smiled and said, "I'm afraid stories are often started by the mistakes people make, good woman."

"Oh." The woman frowned, turning thoughtful. "I hadn't thought of that—but now that you mention it, I suppose there's some truth in it."

Alea sighed with relief, ready to plough ahead.

"Well, telling stories is her work in the world," another woman pointed out. "But it's so obvious a mistake, dearie! Didn't the rest of the villagers warn them and try to talk them out of it?"

"Well . . . um . . . they thought it was none of their business," Alea answered.

"There's some sense in that," a man allowed with an uneasy glance at another man. "Didn't the priestesses tell the father it was wrong?"

"Aye, and the other priests, too!" said an old man.

It struck Gar as an odd but auspicious beginning—and an excellent distraction. As Alea talked, he shifted his weight, taking a step backward—then another and another, until he was at the back of the crowd. There he strolled away with the mildly bored look of one who has heard the tale too often—strolled to the collection box, managed to pick the lock and fish out the white scrap.

It was birch bark with a name scrawled on it in the rough, clumsy letters of someone just learning to read, or who had never troubled to practice writing much. Gar was interested to discover that these peasants could at least read and write one another's names. Beneath the name was the word "bully." Gar wondered if it was a title or an accusation. He slipped the bark back into the box, fastened the crude lock, then went back to listen to the end of Alea's story.

He was just in time to hear her say, "So the priest's son and Cinderella fell in love and bonded."

The adults frowned at one another, obviously feeling something was wrong, but the children burst into a dozen questions.

"Where did they live, though?"

"Did they have children?"

"How long did they stay bonded?"

"They didn't live in the temple, did they?"

Several grim adult faces were nodding, agreeing with the children. Alea guessed at which comment they were nodding and hoped she was right. "Of course the prince called his friends together to build Cinderella her own house," she said.

The grim adult faces cleared as the children cheered.

Alea decided to quit while she was ahead. "So they went into their new house hand in hand—and what they did after that was nobody's business but their own."

The grown-ups laughed and applauded, but the children looked resentful, as though they'd had a sweet taken away.

Gar had to admit that Alea had done a masterful job of adaptation to a local culture.

. . .

On the way out of town the next morning, Gar stiffened and muttered, "Watch that man!"

Alea glanced out of the corner of her eye so she wouldn't seem to be staring. She saw a man in his doorway bending to pick up a scrap of something white that lay on his threshold. Straightening, he studied the scrap, then tore it up angrily and strode off toward the fields, his face flaming.

"What was that all about?" Alea asked out of the side of her mouth.

"I don't know," Gar answered, "but I'd love to find out." As they passed the cottage, he stooped and scooped up the pieces in a single deft motion. "When we're out of town," he muttered, "we'll see how we do with a jigsaw puzzle."

A mile past the town's fields, they stopped, laid out the pieces on a flat rock, and fitted them together.

Alea frowned. "What does it mean?"

"Well, for one thing, our peasant can't read or write very well." Gar pointed to the name that had been very crudely drawn. "I saw the man slip this into the postbox on the common yesterday. Somebody seems to have collected it during the night and given him an answer." He indicated the second set of words, printed much more clearly. They read, "Not a bully. Give one bushel of wheat to the next feast."

"It's a fine," Alea said, frowning, "but for what?"

"False accusation, I'd say." Gar pursed his lips. "I think our peasant was trying to make trouble for an enemy by accusing him."

"He could have simply told the other villagers!"

"Yes, but they would have known if he was right or wrong," Gar said, "and might like the other man well enough to insist on really clear proof. I think our peasant tried to call in people who wouldn't know the facts and wouldn't take sides, but they outsmarted him and learned the truth—very quickly, too."

Alea frowned. "Then who was his judge?"

"The hidden government that I'm sure must be here somewhere!" Gar rose with a tight, intense smile, eyes gleaming. "Perhaps we'll find it at the next village. Let's go!"

Exasperated, Alea watched him stride away. Then she shook her head and started after him.

By midafternoon, they had come out of the flatlands into hilly terrain. The road wound between high banks that rose farther into small mountains.

Gar suddenly stiffened. "Patrol coming!"

Alea stopped, gazing off into space and opening her mind, trying to catch the thoughts he was perceiving.

There they were, and how could she have missed them? They were talking and laughing, but their laughter had a cruel undertone, and they were discussing how they would beat the idiot and amuse themselves with his sister.

"You're getting a reputation," she told Gar.

"I've always wanted to be famous," he answered, "but not this way. It's time for the better part of valor."

"You mean run?" Alea looked about her, baffled. "Where? Those hills will make slow going, and they'll see us a mile away!"

"There are trees on that hillside." Gar pointed to the left.

"If you want to call them that," Alea said sourly.

"They're big enough to hide us, if we bend low," Gar maintained. "It's better than waiting here to try to knock over a dozen well-armed riders with quarterstaves. Let's go while we can!"

10

The roadside brush gave way to low trees quickly. Fortunately, what they lacked in height, they made up in width and density. Gar and Alea had to crouch to stay under the canopy of needles and had to thread their way between gnarled and twisted trunks, but they were hidden.

Then, though, they had to cross an open space between two stands of yew, and heard a shout behind and below them. Alea took a quick glance back and was amazed to see how high they had come already. Below, though, she could see soldiers dismounting, leaving one of their number to hold the horses while the rest dashed into the underbrush to follow the fugitives.

"They're coming," she grated.

"I know." Gar panted. "But . . . no faster than . . . us."

That wasn't much reassurance, but it was better than nothing. Alea forged ahead, breath rasping in her throat—this hillside was steep. Nonetheless, she tried to hurry—but needled branches and twisted roots conspired to slow her down.

Then the trees gave way to grass in a soil so hard underfoot that Alea was amazed anything could grow. There was a shout behind them but she didn't bother to look—she knew the soldiers had seen them.

"They're riders," Gar wheezed. "They're . . . not in shape . . . for climbing."

"Neither are you," Alea snapped, but had to admit she wasn't, either. She wondered if anyone could ever get used to plowing up hillsides this way. She listened to the patrol's thoughts and found them winded, having to force themselves to keep climbing. Then one said to the others, "That man . . . with her . . . he's old!"

"Not too . . . old to . . . climb," another man panted.

"These hillfolk . . . hop uphill like . . . mountain goats," a third soldier rasped.

"Halt," the sergeant said.

Alea didn't, but she could feel the relief from his men.

"We're chasing . . . the wrong . . . travelers," the sergeant gasped.

"There's a . . . woman . . ." a soldier wheezed.

"Not . . . worth it . . ." the sergeant told him. "Other women on . . . the road . . ."

She could feel their silent agreement.

"Back to . . . the horses," the sergeant said.

His men were glad to start back down.

"Keep going," Gar grunted.

"You didn't . . . have to . . . say it," Alea retorted.

Then, suddenly, their feet struck level ground. Gar climbed up onto a mountain ledge and stood staring at it in disbelief. "It's a . . . path!"

"You didn't think . . . we were the only ones . . . ever come . . .

up here . . . did you?" Alea was grateful to climb up onto the ledge, though.

"Frankly . . . yes," Gar said. "At least . . . I didn't expect . . . anyone who wasn't . . . born here."

"They need paths . . . too." But Alea saw what he meant. The path was six feet wide at least and had clearly been hewn out of the rock; she could see the original track had only been three feet across. Someone had widened it—but why?

"Must be something . . . worth seeing . . . up there," Gar said. "Perhaps at least . . . someplace to . . . spend the night."

"Let's look," Alea agreed.

They set out, and since the path was flat and slanted upward across the curve of the hill, it was nowhere nearly as steep as clambering up the hillside would have been. The going was much easier, allowing them to catch their breath. They followed the track around the curve of the hill—and came upon a man sitting at the side of the road.

He sat cross-legged, back perfectly straight, hands on his knees. He had close-cropped gray hair, a lined and weatherbeaten face that was clean shaven, and wore a robe like a longer version of a peasant's tunic, made of the same homespun material.

Alea stopped, staring in amazement. The last thing she would have expected on this mountainside was an old man, and certainly not one who had come all this way up just to sit and admire the view.

On the other hand, any man of his age who came up this path must have to sit down and rest frequently—but looking more closely, she saw that his gaze was unfocused.

Even as she looked, though, his eyes came into focus and his face tilted upward, smile widening. "Good afternoon, my friends. What brings you to this mountain?"

"Refuge," Gar replied.

"The roads aren't terribly safe just now," Alea explained.

"Not even on this mountain, alas." The old man sighed. "Still, if we wished only safety, we should never have been born, should we?"

It struck Alea as an odd thing to say and she could tell from the polite mask that slid over Gar's features that he thought so, too, but he only said, "Some of us didn't have all that much choice in the matter, sir."

"Indeed," the old man agreed. "We live because our parents insisted—or mistook. Still, before we were born, we might have had some choice in the matter."

Gar gave him a thin smile. "If so, good sir, I don't remember it."

"There are very few who do," the old man told him, "and it takes a lifetime's discipline to achieve that." He rose with a fluid grace, amazing in one who had been sitting cross-legged for a long period, and said, "You must not stay your journey for a silly old man, though. Come, let us ascend the mountain together." And he set off as nimbly as a teenager, giving a stream of talk to which Gar listened bemused, and at which Alea marveled.

Then, suddenly, she realized that the old man was listening, nodding encouragement, while she and Gar did the talking. Little by little, he had led them into answering his questions. She tried to stop talking, but his eyes were somehow both compelling and inviting, and she found herself telling him of her parents' deaths and the confiscation of their property, including herself. Near tears, she took refuge in bitterness.

The old man sensed it and turned the question to Gar. "You too have learned to harden your heart, my friend, as a wound develops the hardness of a scar. What cut so deep?"

Alea was suddenly very intent on his answer, not even stopping to wonder why.

"A witch," Gar said, "a woman who enticed me, then humiliated me."

Well. That explained a lot. But why would he tell this to a total stranger and never to her?

Because she was a woman, of course—and because she had touched his heart.

No! Impossible! She turned her attention away from it, or tried to—but the old man had turned to her, no doubt detecting Gar's uneasiness. "And you, young woman? Painful though it may be to be given away as a chattel, there is some deeper hurt within you—and I pity you deeply, for such a pain must be profound indeed!"

Gar turned to her, wide-eyed.

Suddenly self-conscious, she said, "When men treat women as objects, sir, that is surely pain enough."

"Indeed," the old man agreed, "and much more severe it must have been to be so much worse than enough." He turned back to Gar. "But pain that belongs to the past, my friends, must not poison your futures."

"Easily said, sir," Gar said slowly, "but how do you prevent it from doing so?"

"How can you keep yourself from treating new acquaintances as old ones have treated you?" The old man smiled. "Ah, my friends, it is therein that we must have courage, the courage to trust!"

"And to let ourselves be wounded all over again?" Alea was surprised at her own bitterness.

"We must take the risk," the old man said, "or live forever within the shell of ourselves, enclosed and alone, like an oyster who guards his pearl—but what use is that pearl if it is kept always in darkness, never given to the light which alone can show its luster?"

Gar winced; that had touched a nerve somewhere. To hide it, he accused, "You're saying that we must always expose ourselves to attack."

"An attack that may not come," the old man corrected.

"Or may come indeed," Alea said with some heat, "and be worse than any we've known!"

"Therein lies the need for courage," the old man agreed, "but there is never any gain without risk of loss. If we would win friendship, even love, we must open ourselves enough to receive it."

"That is hard to do," Gar said slowly, "when one has been hurt again and again and again."

Alea felt the truth of the statement within herself even as she recognized that Gar's words verified her suspicions. But what hurts had he received?

"You mean that there is no love without trust," she said, "but trust always risks hurt."

The old man nodded. "Therefore love requires courage. An ancient prophet said that if someone strikes you on the cheek, you should turn your face and expose the other cheek for another blow. I think this is what he spoke of, the need to always be open to love no matter how we have been hurt."

"Easy enough to say," Gar said with precise politeness, "but how do we dredge up such courage?"

"By waiting until we find someone else who needs to prove that people can still be trusted," the old man said, "then be patient as they hurt us again and again, ever fearing that we will lash out, ever hoping that they will not."

Alea shuddered. "No human being can have such patience!" She wondered why Gar glanced at her so oddly.

But he turned back to the old man and said, "We must allow someone else to hurt us because they need to learn to trust?"

"Only if they still have the potential to love." The old man raised a forefinger. "It is very hard to tell, because one who can love but who has been hurt guards his heart well behind armor."

Gar winced again, and Alea wondered.

"It is the pearl within the oyster." The old man beamed. "But if the oyster never opens his shell, how can we tell if the pearl is within?"

"Do you not mean that the pearl is within the lotus?" Gar asked with a smile.

"Or is the lotus within the pearl?" the old man returned.

Alea glared at Gar and reminded herself to find out what a lotus was when they were back aboard his ship.

"If the lotus never opens its petals," Gar said, "you can never tell if the pearl is within."

"But if the pearl's surface never clears," the old man riposted, "how can you tell if there is a lotus inside it?"

Gar frowned. "You mean we must have faith."

"Well, you must at least see the sheen of the pearl first," the old man demurred, "to be sure that there *is* a pearl, or at least a lotus. But then, yes, you must have faith in the pearl."

Alea suddenly realized what they were talking about. "And that faith is trust!"

The old man turned and beamed at her. "Exactly. Faith in another human being is trust."

Alea eyed Gar speculatively, found him gazing at her in the same way. Both of them turned away on the instant—so it was just as well that they rounded a curve and saw a broad terrace before them with a thatched hut and half a dozen people in front of it who cried out.

"There he is! The sage!"

"Hail, O Wise One!"

"Give us wisdom to ease our pain, holy man!"

They all bowed and one or two knelt.

"Come, come, now, stand straight and tall, be proud of yourselves!" the old man scolded. "What nonsense is this to kneel to me, who knows no more than a deer or a wolf!"

They straightened up at once, the kneeling ones leaping to their feet.

Alea and Gar stared at the old man with amazement. Then Gar said, with deference, "By your leave, good sir, anyone who can speak of the courage to trust knows considerably more than a deer or a wolf."

"What nonsense!" the old man scoffed. "A deer knows exactly whom it can trust—and whom it cannot."

"You mean the wolf," Gar said.

"Among others. But the wolf, too, knows whom it can trust."

"And whom it cannot?" one of the people asked tentatively.

"Of course."

"But whom can a wolf not trust, O Sage?"

"Other wolves," Gar said slowly.

"And the deer," Alea finished.

The old man's smile was as bright as the sun. "There now, my friends! You knew it all along!"

"Oh, certainly," Gar said softly but with immense sarcasm. "We only needed someone to remind us of it."

"You see?" the old man asked. "I told you I wasn't wise." He turned to the people, who stood waiting eagerly. "What troubles you, my friends?" He pointed at a woman who still looked young. "Your distress is greatest, good woman. What is its cause?"

"I . . . I don't want to talk about it in front of other people, O Sage," the woman said hesitantly.

"Then come into my hut—the walls are thick enough to swallow our voices if we talk softly." The old man beckoned as he went through the doorway. The woman glanced apologetically at the others, then followed.

Gar and Alea stood uncomfortably, shifting their weight from foot to foot and glancing at the others. Finally, to break the silence, Alea asked, "How did he know who was in the most pain?"

"That is a part of his wisdom, of course," a village woman said with a smile. "That is why he is a sage."

Conversation lapsed; after a few minutes, the other people started talking among themselves in low tones.

Alea frowned and nudged Gar. "See those sacks and jugs?"

Gar looked and nodded. "They have brought him gifts."

"We should think about that, too," Alea said slowly.

"We should indeed," Gar agreed, "if for no other reason than that he has given us a place where General Malachi will never think to look."

After a while, the woman came out, looking shaken but resolved. She turned to the old man, saying, "Thank you, O Sage!" She started to bow, then caught herself.

"I thank you, too, for sharing some little part of your life with me," the old man said with a smile. "Go now with an open mind and an open heart, and never stop learning from the world about you."

She nodded, tears in her eyes, and turned to hurry away.

The old man scanned the other petitioners, then pointed at a man and said, "What troubles you?"

"The woman that I love has died in sickbed," the man said, eyes bright with tears. "Why should I go on living?"

"Ah, then," the old man said softly, "that is pain indeed." He sat, folding his legs. "Come, let us recline, for this needs long talk. Tell me, my friends, why you embraced life before you fell in love."

The people looked at one another wide-eyed, then turned back to the sage and sat slowly. The bereaved man said, "I suppose I lived in hope of finding love, O Sage."

"Only in hope?" the old man asked. "Was there nothing to enjoy in life in those days?"

"Food," one person said slowly.

"Festivals," another said.

"Friends," said a third.

Thus it began, and when all the people unrolled their blankets and went to sleep that night, none of them could say that the sage had explained anything, but all of them fell asleep content with their answers.

He is a master of illusion, Gar thought.

Isn't that the same as saying that he knows how to live? Alea returned, and fell asleep.

They breakfasted with the other petitioners, then followed them down the mountainside—but Gar and Alea fell back far enough to talk in low tones as they went.

"So the priestesses and priests aren't the only ones guiding the people," Gar said.

Alea saw where he was heading. "That's not a government! There's a big difference between ruling them and guiding them!"

"Yes," Gar said, "the difference between being driven someplace whether you want to go there or not, and following someone because you want to go where he's going."

"It's a matter of choice," Alea insisted.

"Yes—but if everybody chooses to live in harmony with one another, it has the same effect as government."

"The same effect from a very different cause!"

"True," Gar agreed, "and you're right, it isn't a government—but it does make me wonder why the priests don't object. If there are lots of sages like this one, they're competing with the clergy for control of people's hearts and minds."

Alea frowned, trying to find words to fit her objection. "I never heard him say anything religious."

"True again," Gar admitted, "but it does lessen the priests' control over their people—and if they don't mind that, they're not like any other priests I've ever encountered."

Alea stiffened. "Soldiers coming!"

Gar lifted his head, gazing off into space, and nodded. "Another patrol. At least they're still thinking about the giant half-wit and his sister instead of the old peddler and his daughter."

Alea stood very straight, eyes glazing as she listened to the thoughts below. "They know we're on this mountain but they don't want to come up after us."

"I don't blame them," Gar said. "It's not exactly good terrain for horses."

"They'll have us bottled up here!" Alea protested. "If we don't come down, sooner or later they'll come up!"

"Then we'll have to go down, won't we?" Gar grinned at her.

"How?" she cried, exasperated. "Do you think we can just stroll past them?"

"No," Gar said, "I think we're going to leave the road." He turned aside and ducked into the underbrush.

Alea glared after him, then sighed and followed.

11

Alea caught up to Gar and demanded, "Just how do you think we're going to get down?"

"How do the deer get down?" Gar returned.

She eyed him narrowly. "You've been listening to that sage too much."

"I never disdain good advice," Gar said piously, "no matter the source."

He seemed so sure of himself that Alea felt an irresistible urge to needle. "How do you know it's good advice?"

"Why," Gar said, "when it's the kind of thing I would think of myself, of course."

"You might consider the source," Alea said with dry sarcasm.

"I have been known to make a mistake or two now and then," Gar admitted.

"Such as looking for a government where there isn't any?"

"That's not a mistake until I think I've found one," Gar protested.

Alea turned to stare ahead. "Speaking of finding things . . ."

They had come down into the trees while they had been jibing. Now the pines opened out into a clearing—a new one; there were low stumps all around the edges and three log buildings at its center. Nearby, two young men were sweating over shovels, digging out the roots of one of the stumps. In the cleared ground, other young people were plowing while still others were up on top of the long house, thatching its roof. Others were hanging doors in the dozens of doorways.

"There must be a hundred of them!" Alea said.

Gar nodded, frowning. "That's an awfully high concentration of teenagers—and no chaperones!"

"Oh, I think most of them are in their twenties," Alea demurred.

"Then your eyes are better than mine." Gar lifted his head, stilling for a moment to listen to thoughts, then relaxing. "You're right—they're young, but they're grown."

Alea was listening, too. "Most of them are . . . what did they call it, bonded?"

"They've paired off, anyway," Gar said. "I wonder how many of those pairs will last. . . . Well! Let's test their hospitality."

They went forward to meet the youthful builders.

One of the stump-pullers saw them coming and called out. His fellow worker looked up and dropped his pry bar. They both grabbed their tunics, pulled them on, and came running to meet the new arrivals.

Voices sang out, passing the word from mouth to mouth, and in minutes everyone in the clearing had converged on the companions.

"Peace, my friends, peace!" Gar crackled in his old man's voice. "We've goods aplenty!"

"We have not, I'm afraid," said a plump young woman.

"We're only beginning to plow, as you see, and have little enough that we have gathered from the forest."

"Or hunted and smoked," a young man agreed, "though I expect we could spare a ham or two."

Alea laughed. "We wish to eat, friends, but not to be weighed down! Have you found amber in the streams or rubies at the base of a tree's roots?"

"No such luck, I'm afraid," said a bony brunette. "Still, we can offer you a night's food and lodging in exchange for news and songs!"

Gar glanced at Alea; she nodded and turned to the young woman. "We'll accept your trade, and gladly."

The young people cheered and turned to escort their guests toward the buildings. A few ran on ahead.

As they went, they pointed out their accomplishments proudly. "There's our barn," said a tall young man, "and the two longhouses are our dwellings."

"Crel, you're so silly!" a young woman scoffed. "Anyone can tell that if they've ever been to a new village!"

"To tell you the truth, we haven't," said Alea. "We're from very far away."

"Yes, I thought you had something of an accent," the young woman said with a little frown. "Don't they have new villages where you come from?"

"Rarely," Alea said, "and when they do, they just grow—one person builds a house by a crossroads, then a few years later another person builds nearby, then another and another until you have a village."

"What an odd way of building!" the bony young woman said.

"Now, Honoria," a blond young woman reproved her, "they may like the way they build."

"Well, it's just not sensible, if you ask me." Honoria sniffed.

"We, now, we wait until there're enough young people in three or four villages to start a new one. Then we all march out into the forest together and clear some land for ourselves."

"Don't your parents give you any help?" Alea asked, wide-eyed.

"Oh yes, they all came to help us build the longhouses and the barn when spring began," Crel said, "and they stop by from time to time."

"Which means there's a parent coming to visit every other day," the redhead said with a smile.

"Of course," said a young man who seemed as broad as a door, "they gave us cattle and tools to start with."

"And linens and featherbeds and tableware," the blonde reminded him. "You shouldn't forget that, Umbo."

"Well, no, I shouldn't," Umbo agreed. "After all, we needed them as soon as we arrived here. But once we had built our homes and began plowing, the old folk were happy enough to leave us on our own."

Alea rather doubted that, but she had to admit the parents were being quite restrained about their supervision.

"Of course, we won't be doing any more building until midsummer," Honoria explained, "not until the crops are in and growing. Even then, we'll have to do the hoeing ourselves—won't we, Sylvia?"

"Well, since we don't have any children to do it yet," the blonde said with a smile, "I suppose we shall."

"I've never seen buildings like these," Gar said in his rusty old man's voice. "Why so many doors?"

"Oh, these are just temporary, until we have time to build separate houses," Umbo said. He led Gar and Alea toward the longhouses. "When we do, of course, we can take down the inside walls and have a meeting house—but until then, everyone has their own two rooms."

"With their own outer door." Alea nodded. "Very good. And those inner walls—they're logs, so they're thick?"

"Very thick," Sylvia said, "so they'll keep the heat in."

"When we're done with them, we'll have time to saw the inner walls into planks," Honoria said. "They should be nicely seasoned by then."

"Especially if we hang herbs from the roof beams," Crel said, and everybody laughed.

Spirits were high; everyone seemed to be excited about the adventure of setting up their own village. Several of the villagers proudly showed the travelers their apartments—all the same in size and proportion, but each decorated differently. Some things were the same in every room, such as the herbs truly hanging from the roof beams—and Alea recognized several that she hadn't seen in other villages, so the young folk did have something to trade with, after all. They spent half the day exclaiming over the peddlers' wares but in the end bartered only for needles and pans and a few other useful things; they gazed at the porcelains and figurines with longing but were too poor for luxuries at this stage. Alea resolved to make them presents of several of the exquisite little items when they left.

In the afternoon, the plowers went back into the fields and half a dozen others started to roast a boar and prepare the rest of the evening meal, but all the other villagers sat around and traded stories with Alea while Gar sat watching with twinkling eyes, drinking in every word, every sound. He had to admit that Alea did a much better job adapting Snow White and Siegfried than she had with Cinderella—but then, she knew the pitfalls now. He was intrigued to see how well the villagers responded to the notion of a hero fighting a dragon and wondered if there had been local monsters in the early days of the colony.

Then it was time for dinner, which everyone ate with laughter and bright conversation. Alea noticed a great deal of flirting and wondered if perhaps some of the pairings weren't really settled yet. She did see some jealous glances and wondered if the colony would survive until its members had sorted out who should stay with whom.

"What if you find you're paired with someone you don't like after all," she asked Sylvia, "or if you fall out of love?"

"Oh, that happens all the time when you're our age," Sylvia said. "If two people can't get along or the woman falls in love with somebody else, she just puts the man's gear outside the door and that's the end of it."

"The end?" Alea stared. "Doesn't the man object?"

"Of course not." Sylvia looked at her strangely. "The house is the woman's, after all."

"Even though the man built it?"

"We *all* build the houses," Sylvia said. "Isn't that how it's done in your homeland?"

"No, it's not," Alea said, "but I'm beginning to think it should be. What if it's the man who falls out of love?"

"Oh, then he takes his things and moves into the bachelors' house," Sylvia said. "That's what the other longhouse is for."

All in all, Alea liked the system.

When dinner was done, she volunteered to help the dozen people who did the washing up and putting away while someone brought out a small set of bagpipes and others brought out flutes and fiddles. The young folk danced for an hour or more, laughing and chatting and flirting. Then as the sky darkened, they went indoors—some to the bachelors' house, many couples to the main longhouse.

"There is one dwelling for two still empty," Crel offered.

"No, thank you," Gar said in his oldest voice. "I think my daughter would rather sleep by herself. Wouldn't you, my dear?"

"Of course I would, Papa," Alea said demurely while she directed a thought at Gar—that it was a very good thing he hadn't accepted the first invitation.

He looked up at her in surprise; then his eyes crinkled in amusement. He disguised it by covering his mouth for a yawn.

"Yes, I don't manage late nights as well as I used to. A bed would be very welcome right now."

Alea noticed that he hadn't said whose.

Alea woke in the night, wondering what had roused her. She looked around the small room the young folk had given her—the glow of starshine through the window and the answering glow from the hearth both illuminating a small table with a jug and a basin, the chair beside it with her clothes draped over it, and the great eyes with crinkled corners that seemed to glow in the darkness of the room.

Alea sat bolt upright, fear churning upward to become a scream—but before it emerged, she recognized the huge globe of fur and the toothy grin. She relaxed somewhat and thought, *So you can come indoors, too. I thought you were creatures of the forest.*

This village is very much in the forest, Evanescent reminded her. If it were in a town, now, there might have been somebody awake, and I would have had to have been much more circumspect.

Alea had a notion that in that case, "circumspect" would have meant lulling people to sleep telepathically. *You could give a body some warning. I can't breathe well with my heart in my throat.*

You know I mean you no harm. Evanescent seemed spectacularly undisturbed by the notion. Besides, rapid heartbeats and deepened breathing increase the health of your kind.

Only when they come from exercise, Alea thought caustically. It seemed amazing to her that she hadn't thought of the native alien since their first encounter. Why, she might have forgotten Evanescent completely!

Then she realized that she had.

I don't like anyone playing with my mind, she thought, keeping the anger an undertone.

What of your heart? Evanescent replied. **Do you still deny that the big one is your mate?**

I deny it most strenuously! Even Alea thought that was a strange word, but it was out and there was no helping it.

Then why do you aid him so?

I don't aid him—I'm sharing his adventures and letting him aid me!

To what purpose?

To learn—to see new things—to meet new kinds of people! The glory of it seized Alea all over again—the tremendous excitement of actually being on a different world!

What have you learned, then?

A fantastic amount. The whole complex of new and strange ways of thinking and behaving jumped into Alea's mind in an instant. She tried to steady them, to focus them; the easiest was to say what she hadn't learned. *But we still have not found their government.*

What a strange concept that is! Evanescent marveled. **Ordering and making methodical the ways of living beings! Is it not simpler to let each follow her own path?**

People don't work that way, Alea explained. *We're social creatures—we have to have others of our kind about.*

Strange, very strange. Evanescent seemed delighted by the notion. **But why is your mate so upset not to find this government that he sees as some sort of great barren tree?**

He thinks it is the only way to save people from famine, disease, and oppression. Without it, he sees only that strong people will hurt weaker people and make them miserable.

There is some truth to that, Evanescent mused, but a government like that which General Malachi wishes to make would hurt and oppress people even more.

Gar thinks that is what happens where there is no better form of government to stop such a man.

Ah! His true concern, then, is to prevent the suffering of his fellow creatures!

Why . . . yes, I suppose so. Alea hadn't thought of it in quite that way before.

And he seeks to protect the people from such as General Malachi, Evanescent thought, exulting. He must seek out the Scarlet Company then.

He has tried, Alea thought. *He cannot find it.*

Find it for him, then. The alien grinned, sending shivers down Alea's spine. What kind of mate are you?

Not a mate at all! Alea fairly screamed—in her mind, of course.

Seek to find the Scarlet Company for him, Evanescent advised, but seek to know your own heart first.

The coals flared up on the hearth and Alea turned to look at them, heart pounding—but the flame died down as quickly as it had risen, and she sagged back onto the strange bed, wondering that so minor a thing should have wakened her. Well, she could find sleep again easily enough. She looked around the small, empty room once, to remind herself where she was, then rolled over on her side and closed her eyes.

There was an undercurrent of excitement at breakfast the next day. When they were done eating, people circulated, talking with one another, and Alea began to feel guilty. Finally she went to Sylvia and said, "We're planning to go on with our journey. Your people really mustn't stay home just for us."

Sylvia stared at her in astonishment, then laughed and caught her hands. "Don't feel badly—it's not you we're waiting for."

"Who, then?" Alea asked in surprise.

"The priestess! She's coming to bless the fields this morning! That's why the plowers had to finish yesterday even though they were dying to stay and coax you into telling another story!"

Gar looked up with interest, then came tottering over. "Surely this will be a festive event, Daughter. Let us stay to honor the goddess."

"Of course, Father." Alea wondered if the goddess would really feel honored by Gar's curiosity.

The priestess arrived in midmorning, accompanied by two junior priestesses and two priests who led a cart pulled by a donkey and filled with bulging sacks tied at the mouth. She smiled at the greetings of the young folk and accepted their plaudits. When she and her entourage had rested and taken some wine, she rose, assuming dignity like a garment, and intoned, "Are all the fields plowed?"

Honoria stepped forth, a clean white robe belted over her everyday homespun. "Indeed, Reverend Lady, they are."

"Let us go to them, then." The priestess spoke with the cadence of ritual, then turned to glide toward the fields. Her acolytes followed, a man and a woman to each side and a little behind in an inverted V. The people trooped along, singing a tune that managed to be both solemn and joyful. With a shock, Gar recognized the ode from Beethoven's Ninth Symphony.

When they came to the plowed land, the acolytes fanned out to the sides and brought shoulder bags out from under their cloaks. Slipping the straps over their heads, they marched down the furrows, sprinkling powder with circular sweeps of their hands.

Don't you dare! Alea thought at Gar.

But it's so hard to resist, Gar thought back.

Alea turned to glare daggers at him and saw that he had somehow managed to hobble to the fore, swinging his hands in time to the music—and could he help it if the swing of his hand crossed the spray of powder?

Yes, of course he could help it—and had. Alea saw the hand go into his pocket even as he slowed, as a tired old man would, and let younger people pass him, dropping back toward the rear of the crowd.

Is nothing sacred? she thought angrily.

Of course, Gar replied, *and I can tell you exactly what's in my people's sacred oils and powder and incense. Surely there's no sacrilege in my finding out what's in theirs.*

True enough on the face of it, but somehow Alea felt that the spirit was lacking.

The procession paced off every furrow of each of the four fields, then came back to the common between the longhouses.

"You have plowed well," the priestess intoned. "How shall you plant?"

"Soybean in the northern field," Sylvia replied, with the same ceremonial cadence, "maize in the southern, tomatoes in the eastern, and potatoes in the western."

What are you smiling about now? Alea demanded.

Only because none of those crops was known in medieval Europe, Gar thought in answer.

Alea felt angry without knowing why. *Who says these people had to be modeled after Europeans?*

No one, Gar admitted. *In fact, a lot of their styles are a very nice blend of every early culture I've heard about.*

Alea felt the glow of a minor triumph.

"What will you plant next year?" the priestess intoned, and with a start of surprise, Alea realized one of the junior priestesses was writing down the answers.

"Maize in the northern field," Sylvia replied, with the same ceremonial cadence, "tomatoes in the southern, potatoes in the eastern, and soybeans in the western."

"What shall you offer the goddess to ward against weeds?"

Alea saw Gar tense up. *What worries you?*

Human sacrifice, Gar thought back, *especially since they have a couple of handy strangers to offer.*

"We shall plant pumpkins and squash amid the corn," Sylvia answered, "whose broad leaves shall stifle weed-shoots—and of course we shall hoe."

Alea saw Gar relax and thought a gibe: *Don't you feel silly now?*

No, I feel alive, Gar thought back, *and very nice it is, too.*

You should feel ashamed of yourself, Alea rebuked him. *Why would you suspect something so gruesome of such nice people?*

They are *Neolithic, after all.*

Alea's lips tightened. *Don't you think you should apologize?*

How, without letting them know what I was thinking?

"How shall you ward your crops from ravening insects?" the priestess demanded.

"We shall plant blooming asterones and blossoming meromies," Sylvia answered.

Alea frowned. *What are asterones and meromies?*

Flowers that the original colonists brought, Gar replied. *I have heard of them—they were first bred on Terra when her people began to colonize other planets, and a great boon they've been to farmers all over the Terran Sphere.*

"Well done, daughter of the goddess," the priestess said. "Do thus every year."

Crop rotation and central coordination of production, Gar thought, *but it's not a government.*

Well, of course not! Alea thought indignantly. *They're choosing to do it.*

Choosing to do as they've been taught, Gar qualified.

There's no crime in that!

None at all, Gar agreed.

Why did Alea feel she had lost another round? Gar was insufferable! Perhaps she shouldn't suffer him after all. These people seemed nice enough; perhaps she should stay with them, and let Gar go on without her.

For some reason, the mere thought raised panic in her.

The priestess raised her arms and turned slowly so that she swept all the villagers with her gaze as she intoned, "Well have you begun, well may you continue! The blessing of the goddess be upon you, and upon all that your earth and you yourselves shall bear!" She lowered her arms and in a more normal voice cried out, "Celebrate, children! Celebrate life and the gifts of the goddess!"

The villagers shouted with joy, and the music and dancing began.

The priestess and her entourage left in midafternoon with a cartful of empty sacks. As dusk gathered, Alea came back from the dancing to her "aged parent," sat down by him, and asked, "Did Herkimer analyze the powder yet?" She knew he carried a dagger whose sheath transmitted and identified the molecules of any substance by sonic reflection and beamed that identification up to the spaceship.

"He did," Gar told her. "It was mostly nitrates of organic origin—nothing that a real Neolithic society couldn't have manufactured, but something that none of them would ever have thought of."

"It was fertilizer, then?"

Gar nodded. "Nice way to get them off to a good start. After all, they don't have enough cows or horses to do it the more primitive way. I have a notion it's a good supplement even when they do have a full complement of livestock."

"You're trying to tell me the priestess isn't working any real magic," Alea accused.

Gar stared at her in surprise. "I certainly am not! I didn't even think of it as magic—just a ritual to focus and direct people, make them feel the rightness and purpose in their work, and give them confidence in the outcome."

"Only what any religious ritual gives?" Alea said slowly.

"Well, yes, but that's just the side effect," Gar said. "The real purpose is worship, of course, and I saw a great deal of sincerity in that."

There wasn't much to argue about there. Still, his skepticism seemed vaguely blasphemous. "You mean you're not trying to say their religion is a sham?"

"No, I'm not," Gar said, "no more than the medieval monasteries and convents were shams simply because they kept alive a little of the learning of the Greeks and Romans."

Alea could accept that—and felt a bit better for it.

"Still, I do think it was very clever of the original colonists," Gar said. "One more way of keeping alive the benefits of civilization in a Neolithic society."

Alea bridled once more. "You mean you think they were cheating again."

"Of course."

They left the next morning, leaving presents of flower vases, amber, and figurines, to the delight of their hosts. The young people waved as they left, calling good-byes and making them promise to return someday. When the trees swallowed up the clearing, Alea stopped waving and turned back to Gar. "They're

frowning with the effort of remembering. "They were a nation of sorcerers, weren't they?"

"I would prefer to think of them as wizards and magicians."

"What's the difference?"

"In my homeland," Gar said slowly, "sorcerers work evil magic. Wizards and magicians work good magic."

"What's the difference?"

"Good magic defends people and helps them to grow and prosper. Evil magic hurts people and destroys them."

Alea thought that over, then asked, "So you only know the two by the effects?"

"No. There's a matter of what the magic-worker means to do, and what symbols and words he uses to bring it about. A sorcerer uses symbols such as skulls, blood, and knives—things of death and pain—but a good magician uses such things as plants and feathers, earth and water."

"This Kullervo—he was a sorcerer, then?"

"He could be rather unpleasant," Gar said slowly, "but he was reared as a captive and a slave and grew up to become vengeful and vindictive. That was what brought him down eventually—that and being in the wrong place at the wrong time, and having grown up far away from his own people, so that he didn't know them when he saw them."

"Did they want him when he came home?" Alea asked, her voice low.

"At first," Gar said.

He was silent for a few moments. Alea waited.

"One man, long ago, said that when you seek revenge," Gar said, "you begin to destroy yourself." He thought for a moment, then added, "It was the only truly wise thing he ever said."

"He wasn't a sage, then?"

"No, he was a governor, a man who ruled, though he had to share the authority. Rulers may be intelligent and shrewd, but they use their minds to gain power, not to try to understand the universe and our place in it. I think very few of them are really wise. Maybe that's why we remember the ones who are."

Insight came, and Alea said, "So you don't seek revenge."

"No, I don't." Gar smiled. "I seek the greatest good of the greatest number instead. I think that if I had stayed home and sought revenge I wouldn't have accomplished much else." He thought a moment again, then said, "Not that I'm sure I have after all."

"There are tens of thousands of people on half a dozen worlds who think you have," Alea said. That much, at least, he had told her of his past.

The next village greeted them with the usual delight; again, they were the occasion for an impromptu holiday. Here the people used the long winter days to weave luxurious woolens and linens as fine as silk. They were glad to trade, and Gar and Alea came away feeling they had made a considerable profit with the last of their porcelains and figurines.

One young woman was so obviously near delivery that Alea commented on it to an older woman, who glanced anxiously at the mother-to-be. "It's her first. We're all praying for an easy delivery."

"Of course," Alea said. "Is there reason to worry for her? More than for any first-time mother, that is."

"Only that our midwife has died and her apprentice has never delivered a baby by herself. She's quite nervous."

"Small wonder," Alea said with a smile. "Well, I've helped with many a birth, and I've learned a thing or two about troubles, so call me if there's need."

The woman looked at her in surprise, then smiled and pressed her hand. "Bless you, good soul! My name is Masha."

"Mine is Alea." She returned the pressure.

"We won't have need to call you, please the goddess—but if we do, be sure we shall."

They did.

12

The call came in the middle of the night; the messenger was a twelve-year-old girl who was pale with fright. "Please, mum, an' it please you, would you come to Agneli? She's most horrible took with the baby, mum!"

Gar started up from his pallet by the fire. "I can . . ."

"No you can't," Alea said firmly. "In a village like this, birthing is for women only—unless something is drastically wrong."

"But I am a physician . . ." the old man voice croaked.

"Then heal yourself," Alea snapped. "If we need a cesarean, I'll send for you."

"Are you sure . . ."

"Don't worry, I gleaned a great deal from Herkimer's memory," Alea assured him. "Midwifery was the first topic I searched."

"It was?" Gar stared.

"Of course," Alea said. "I had to make sure your man-made computer hadn't ignored women, didn't I? Go back to sleep, my friend."

Gar smiled, obviously warmed by the term "friend." Alea gave him another smile, then turned and went.

Agneli screamed as Alea came in; her impulse was to turn and go, but she knew the young woman hadn't even seen her. Instead, she marched straight up to the bedside and asked, "How long has she been in labor?"

"Since dusk." Her mother looked up, face drawn and haggard. She sat beside Agneli, mopping her brow with a cool cloth.

"That is not so long." Alea sat beside Agneli.

"No, but the babe is nearly to the birth canal, yet keeps pulling back."

"I don't blame her," Alea said with a wry smile. "If I had so warm and safe a place to live, I doubt I would choose to leave it." She put her hands on Agneli's belly and gazed off into space.

The mother started to say something, but one of the other women touched her hand. "Shh! She reads the child."

The mother stared in awe, then closed her mouth.

Alea listened to the baby's mind. There were no words, of course, only raw emotions—fear and, as Agneli screamed with the strength of the contraction, the feeling of something pinching, of fainting . . .

The spasm passed and Agneli went limp, gasping. Alea's gaze focused on the mother. "The child is coming feet first with the umbilical cord between its legs. Worst, it is pinched between the babe's hip and the mother's bone. Whenever she moves toward the canal, it pinches closed, and the child cannot breathe."

"The child will suffocate!" the mother exclaimed.

"The child will not come out either, if we cannot free that cord," Alea said.

"But how?" the mother whispered, eyes huge.

"I need a wooden wand," Alea said, "two feet long, with a notch on the end."

One of the women went out. While she was gone, Alea held Agneli's hand and helped soothe her through the contractions. Between them, she thought, *Gar.*

Aye?

He couldn't have been asleep—he must have been waiting. *You have heard?*

Would I eavesdrop?

Stop being silly! The umbilical cord is caught between the baby's legs and the inner rim of the pelvis. Can you loosen it with telekinesis?

I think so, Gar answered; then his thoughts blurred.

The neighbor came back in with a peeled willow wand half an inch thick with a small fork on the end, carefully smoothed. "I carved with haste. Will it do?"

"Admirably," Alea said. "Boil it for three minutes."

The woman turned away to the kettle. "How shall I know three minutes?"

"One hundred eighty beats of your pulse."

A few minutes later, Alea was pretending to probe with the wand while she listened to the baby's mind, one hand on the mother's belly. She felt the baby move farther back inside, and its thoughts cleared as oxygen flooded its blood. Then it descended again.

Success, Gar's voice said inside her head.

Alea withdrew the wand. "Pray to the goddess."

Agneli stiffened, crying out.

"I see the feet!" a woman cried.

"And the child still breathes," Alea said triumphantly.

"Praise the goddess!" the mother said fervently.

Alea surprized herself by muttering a quick prayer of thanks to Freya. Then she thought, *Thank you, Gar.*

There were no words in return, only a quiet feeling of satisfaction and pride. Well, at least he had used his powers to a good purpose.

Time blurred then, seeming both far too long and all too short—but at last Alea held a fully formed, beautiful female child in her hands. Its mouth opened, gaped, then let out a thin wail of protest.

Alea smiled. "May your complaint be in vain, little one— and may your life be wonderful."

One of the other women cut and tied the cord, then took the child from her to wash. Alea said, "Who shall tell the father?"

An embarrassed silence fell and no one would meet her eyes.

"What?" Alea frowned. "Does he not acknowledge his responsibility?"

"They have not bonded," the mother said, "and Agneli has not told us his name."

The tension in the room was sudden and great. The same thought burned in everyone's mind—that she had been seduced by someone else's husbandman.

Then the neighbor laid the baby on Agneli's breast and said gently, "The child is come, Agneli, and needs her father's protection. Will you not now tell us his name?"

"It . . . it was Shuba," Agneli caressed the baby at her breast with a faint but growing smile.

The tension released, to be replaced by a new and grim one. "He must provide for the child," said the neighbor.

But Shuba refused. There in the dawn light, Agneli's mother held out the child to him, but he turned away. "Agneli refused to bond with me and told me she had fallen in love with someone else. Let him feed her and her child!"

A soft murmur ran though the villagers—not surprise, but recognition. Alea wondered if the young woman had been too obvious in showing her attraction to the other boy.

Now Agneli's father stepped forward. "They never lay together. The child is yours."

"I will not bond with a woman who loves me not!"

"No one says that you should," the father said quietly, "and all the village will support the child if we must. But you should give the greatest part of that support."

"If she were in love with me, I would." Shuba glanced at the baby, and for a moment longing filled his face.

Then he turned away. "I will not pay for a child raised by another man!"

Shuba's father stepped up beside him. "It is not justice that he do so."

Agneli's father's face hardened; his hands balled into fists. "It is not justice that Shuba fail to provide for the child he has begotten."

The village was silent and tense. Then another man stepped up beside Shuba's father. "He offered and was refused. It is not just."

A fourth man stepped up beside Agneli's father. "It is just and proper to support your own child."

One by one, the men of the village lined up on one side or the other. The women began to protest and their pleas grew to demands, louder and louder. The men held silence, their faces hard.

Gar stood leaning on his staff, tense as a bowstring. Alea spared an angry glare for him. Did he think they were going to invent a government on the spur of the moment?

There was a sudden commotion at the back of the crowd. The women parted and the sage strolled in, turning from side to side as he passed between the two lines of men, smiling at each. He came in silence, but the tension of the people lessened visibly.

At the center of the lines, the sage sat down on the ground and looked up at the antagonists. "Good day to you all, my friends."

Muttered greetings from shamed faces answered him.

"You are well come, O Sage," Shuba's father said. "To what do we owe the pleasure?"

"Why, to the Scarlet Company, my friend," the sage said.

Gar stiffened so suddenly that Alea half expected him to break in two.

"When I came out to greet the sun," the sage said, "there was a trouble sign scratched in the dust before my door and the character for your village next to it."

"How did they know so quickly?" one man muttered.

"They know everything, of course!" another man hissed. "Be still! I want to hear the sage!"

"What is the cause of the trouble?" the sage asked.

Shuba's father sat on his heels beside the man. "My son got Agneli with child—but she refused to bond, for she fell in love with another man who did not love her. The babe was born this night past and Agneli finally named the father, but Shuba refuses to acknowledge the child."

"What he begot, he should husband!" Agneli's father insisted, sitting beside the sage.

One by one, the men sat down in a circle. The women heaved sighs of relief.

"The custom is that the village rears a child whose mother breaks the bond with the father," the sage said thoughtfully.

"That is so, O Sage," Shuba said, "but I have not had the pleasure of living with Agneli for even one day!"

"You had the pleasure of sleeping with her for a night," one of the other young men said darkly.

"I did not!" Shuba turned to him. "I lay with her for an hour, no more! She would not stay to fill my arms in the night or to greet the sun with me!"

The men all murmured together.

"It is true what he says."

"Aye—fornicating is only a part of the pleasure of lovemaking."

"The smallest part, in some ways."

"It is such great pleasure to wake and find the woman in your arms."

Alea's opinion of this culture's men soared. She locked gazes with Gar, who was looking impressed, too.

"And do you wish to deny yourself the pleasure of talking with the child when she is three?" the sage asked.

Shuba started to answer, then hesitated.

"When she is eight," the sage asked, "will she come to show you the treasure of a nestling who has fallen? Or will she turn away from you as you now turn away from her?"

"I will not sleep in the same house as she," Shuba protested, but his face already showed regret.

"That you will not," the sage agreed, "but few of us can have everything we wish, or gain as much joy from it as we expect. It is better to take what happiness we can, to delight in the little pleasures of life while we wait for the greater."

Shuba glanced at the baby with longing but still protested, "Even if I do not acknowledge her, I shall contribute to her rearing as much as any man in this village."

"So you shall," said the sage, "but no more. Why then should she bring you her joys and woes to share more than to any other man?"

Shuba bowed his head, scowling at the ground. All the men were silent.

"The true conflict, then, is between yourself and yourself," the sage said gently. "Which do you wish more—the love of a child or vengeance for a slight?"

Shuba still scowled.

"Men are born with empty hearts," the sage said. "We fill them with love and joy, hate and pain, as we grow. The first pair makes the heart limber and light, the second makes it hard and heavy. Will you spend your life with a jewel in your chest, or a lump of lead?"

Slowly and reluctantly, Shuba lifted his head, then nodded. "The babe is mine."

As they pulled on their packs, Alea said softly, "It seems there isn't always a need for a judge and a court."

"Isn't there?" Gar looked her straight in the eye. "I thought I saw both back there."

"I saw only a teacher guiding people in living," Alea said sharply.

"Which is what a judge should perhaps be."

"But rarely is! And what of his bailiffs, his guards? Where were they?"

"Ah—the police." Gar nodded. "No one saw them, did they? But they were there nonetheless. Someone told the Scarlet Company, and they told the sage."

"The Scarlet Company is a bailiff?"

"A sentry, at least," Gar said.

Then they had to drop the issue because Shuba and his parents came up to them with half the village behind them. He held out cupped hands to Alea. "I thank you, lady, for the life of my child."

Alea almost told him to thank Gar, too, but stopped herself just in time. "You are welcome, my friend. I share your joy."

"May you always do so!" Shuba said. "To remind you of it, here is a gift of my own carving."

He opened his hands, and Alea caught her breath in wonder. A small golden bird sat on his palm; its eyes were tiny rubies and its wings were edged in pure gems.

"I cannot accept so rich a gift for only a few hours' labor," she protested.

"For the life of my daughter, rather." Shuba pressed it into her hands. "Take it, please, lady—and when you look upon it, breathe a small prayer for Agneli and myself."

She looked into his eyes, saw the longing there, and realized that no matter whom Agneli fancied, Shuba still loved her. "I shall pray for you both," she promised, "for all three."

Now Shuba's mother stepped up beside him. "Hide it well within your pack, lady, for General Malachi's men still prowl the roads, and though they may call themselves soldiers, they are still every bit the bandits they were before his rise."

"The sage told us that he has conquered yet another village," one of the men said, frowning.

"So you know of this bandit captain," Gar said in his rusty old voice.

"Know of him! I should say so!" said an old woman. "Why, the whole land between the big lake and the forest talks of nothing else!"

"Then you know he's bossing around the people of three villages now?"

"Four, the last I heard," a big man grunted. "Like to see him try his tricks here!"

"I wouldn't." The woman next to him shuddered. "You're a

strong man, my Corin, but you can't stand against a hundred on horseback!"

"A hundred? Come, Phillida!" Corin scoffed. "Surely he doesn't have so many!"

"That and more, if the tales I've heard are true," Gar said in his gravelly voice. "Who made this Malachi a general, anyway?"

If he had been hoping to hear about a government that Malachi had been too proud to mention, he was sadly disappointed.

"He did that himself," Phillida answered. "The tale tells that he was outlawed for bullying in his own village, but he proved a bigger bully than any knew, and soon he bullied all the bandits in the forest."

"Then he came out of his woodlands," an old man said, "came out with a hundred bandits at his back and started forcing the people of his village to obey him."

"His bandits drove the villagers before them to take the blows of a second village," another man said, "then conquered that village, then a third, and the Scarlet Company hasn't stopped them yet."

Gar bit his lip in an agony of curiosity. Alea saw and took pity on him. She told the villagers, "We're from very far away. What is this Scarlet Company? We've been hearing about it for a month, but no one's told us what it is."

"You don't have a Scarlet Company in your home?" The old woman stared at them. "Who holds your bullies in check, then?"

Remembering Midgard, Alea said bitterly, "No one—or at least, only bigger bullies."

The people shuddered, looking at one another. "What a horrible place!" said the old man, and Phillida added, "No wonder you left there!"

"I only wonder that I didn't leave it sooner." Of course, Alea couldn't have left her home planet until Gar invited her aboard his spaceship, but they didn't need to know that. Reminder of obligation made her feel more prickly and she asked again. "So tell me what this Scarlet Company is."

"Why, it's a company of people who stop bullies from hurting peaceable people like us, of course," said another man.

"Who are they?" Gar tried to hide the keenness of his interest. "Where can I find them?"

The whole crowd laughed at that, and one man said, "Why, everywhere and nowhere, peddler! No one's ever seen a man or woman of the Scarlet Company—except the bosses whom they've killed, and those folk knew nothing of any others!"

"It's secret, then?" Gar quavered.

"Secret as the stars in the daytime!" the old woman said. "You know they're there, but you can't ever see them. When the land grows dark, though, there they are to give you light and hope."

"Lucky you are to have them," Gar said.

"Aye, lucky unless you've tried to bully someone, or accused someone else falsely." The old man looked at the others about him with a toothless grin; one or two flushed and looked away. "Me, I did that once. I was angry with a neighbor, so I marked a bit of bark against him and slipped it into the collection box on the common." He shook his head ruefully, eyes gazing off into the past. "I found their reply on my doorstep and took it to the priest to read. They knew me for the liar I was and bade me give five jugs of ale to the next village feast."

Gar frowned. "Who empties the collection boxes?"

"No one knows," the old woman said. "No one's ever seen—or if they have, they've been wise enough not to tell."

"They guard their secret well," Gar said with ill-disguised disgust.

"Very well," the old man agreed, "and fools would we be to try to spy them out."

They waved good-bye as they went down the road, then waved again—but as soon as they were out of the villagers' hearing, Alea said, "Will you stop looking for the Scarlet Company now?"

"I make no promises," Gar said, "but I certainly won't stop looking for the government. I will say, though, that this is the first time in my life I've ever had to look for one. Usually the government comes looking for me."

Suddenly, he bowed his head, clutching it with his right hand while he leaned on his staff with his left.

"What is it?" Alea cried. "Are you ill?"

"Thoughts," Gar gasped, "panic . . ."

Alarmed, Alea turned her attention to the world of thought—and the terror and pain almost drove her to her knees.

13

It was the massed fear of fifty people mixed with images of fire and blood, and throughout and above it reverberated shouted threats and gloating insults, brutal men exulting in the fear and pain they inspired.

"The young people," Alea gasped, "the new village . . ."

"Malachi found them." Gar straightened and turned back. "We must help them!" He strode away down the road.

Alea hurried to catch up.

They had only gone a mile when they saw a plume of smoke rising out of the distant mountain forest.

Alea caught Gar's arm with a cry of despair. In her mind, the image of fire consumed all others and terror drowned all emotions but pain.

"I can't wait," Gar snapped. "See if the villagers can lend you a horse."

A loud report sounded next to her, like a stick breaking, only much louder. Alea turned to ask what he meant, but he was gone. She stared in fright for a moment, then felt anger rising. He had kept some mental power secret, hadn't told her of it! She would make his ears ring for that.

First, though, she had to reach him—and had to go to the new village as fast as she possibly could. She started running.

They loaned her a horse—all of their horses, in fact, as well as their carts and themselves, leaving only a few adults behind to care for the children. The riders galloped up the mountain road, sweeping Alea with them, leaving the slower carts and the people afoot to come as best they could. Even so, it was almost noon before they rode into the charred timbers that had been a village only a night before.

Alea stared around her at the emptiness of the smoking ashes, sick foreboding filling her. "Where is everyone?"

"Taken," Shuba said, his mouth a grim line. "Stolen. Kidnapped, the men to be used as living shields against the arrows of the next village General Malachi means to take, and the women for . . . slavery."

He didn't have to tell Alea what that meant. She knew, and fury filled her. "Out upon this foul bandit! We might come in time to free the young ones!"

Then they heard the moan coming from the smoking ruins and the cursing that answered it.

Alea slipped down from her saddle and ran around a heap of charred wood to find a jumble of timbers and Gar so smeared with ashes and soot that she wouldn't have known him if it hadn't been for his height, straining against the weight of a huge blackened timber.

Alea stared only a second, then whirled to the village men. "Help him! Throw those beams aside! Find whoever calls!" She turned back and ran to help Gar.

The men were beside her on the instant, throwing timbers

aside and using sticks to lever away those that were still smoking. In a hollow beneath them, they found a young man, dried blood caked on brow, shoulder, and tunic, covered with ashes but still alive. "Bless you, neighbors!" he groaned. "Are any . . . any of the others . . . ?"

"We'll find out soon enough," Shuba said grimly, and led a party away to search while Alea knelt beside the youth to do what she could for his burns and wounds.

An hour later, they had scattered all the charred timbers and were covered with soot—but they had found two girls and four boys whom the raiders must have thought too badly wounded to survive. They weren't far wrong—Alea and Gar worked frantically, she with her hands, he with his mind, closing slashed blood vessels, regrowing nerve tissue and burned skin. Gar prodded the bodies into making more blood as Alea trickled water past parched lips and over swollen tongues. The two worst injured died in their arms and Alea began to feel a sullen hatred toward General Malachi and his men.

So did three of the survivors; the fourth, a young man, only gazed off into space, his face enpty. Alea focused her mind on his thoughts and shuddered when she found only a smooth, featureless blank. His mind had retreated into a corner of his brain and buried itself in memories of childhood, disconnected entirely from his body.

The two other young men and the young woman swore vengeance even as they groaned from the pain of their wounds.

"He has taken Felice!" one of the boys grated, then ground his teeth against the pain. When the spasm passed, he panted, "They mowed down Ethera and Genald, Hror and Venducci! They drove the rest like cattle—I saw blood from their swords, saw one strike Theria backhanded when she dared to rebuke him!"

"They fought like beasts," the young woman said with deadly

calm. "They laid about them with their clubs and knives and didn't care whom they struck, or where. They threw torches into the longhouses and struck our friends down as they ran out to escape the flames."

"There was nothing of fairness or rightness in the way they fought," growled the other young man. "They kicked crotches and struck from behind—and this against people on foot when they were mounted! They are brutes, not men!"

"You gave as well as you could, Crel," the young woman said, a little life coming into her voice. "I saw you standing over Eralie with your quarterstaff until that brute struck you down from behind."

"Eralie!" the lad groaned, burying his face in his hands. "I'll be revenged on them for this, I swear it!"

"I don't know how," the other young man swore, "but I'll find a way to cut their throats and break their heads!"

"I'll hold them while you cut, Borg," Crel said, then bleated with the pain of his wounds. "I'll see them burn as they burned us!"

"There has to be a way to hurt them," the young woman said with the intensity of hatred, "and when I find it, I'll watch each of them die screaming—or at least their general!"

Alea started to tell them that trying to revenge would only destroy them but caught herself and pressed her lips shut at the last second. Later they might respond to such an idea—months later. Right now, though, they needed whatever purpose they could find to give them the will to live.

Shuba and his neighbors took the young people home to nurse while they waited for the priestess to come to heal them, and to tell their own villagers of the horror they had seen. Alea and Gar watched them go. Shaken to her core, Alea mourned their former hosts. "Those cheerful, openhearted, generous young people we saw only two days ago, with everything to live for and every minute an adventure—they're as burned out as their village now, grim and filled with bitterness!"

"Crel's wrong when he called them animals," Gar said grimly. "Wolves and bears only kill bodies, but these monsters have maimed their souls!"

"If the Scarlet Company is so good at stopping bullies," Alea said bitterly, "what are they waiting for?"

"Good question," Gar said. "Let's find them and ask."

They found a town instead—a real, genuine town, or at least a village large enough to qualify as one. Actually, it looked more like a collection of villages than an actual town.

"You'd better bury that charcoal robe and take a bath before you go in there," Alea warned.

Gar looked down at his doctor's robe, the hem ragged and charred. "You're right—I must look like a fugitive from a coal mine." He turned back to her. "I'm sorry to burden you so long with such a sight. I hadn't realized."

"No, you wouldn't, would you?" Alea asked. "You had others' suffering to worry about—and so had I. But you might have told me you could vanish from my side and appear miles away."

"Ah—that." Gar had the grace to look embarrassed. "Yes, well, I was going to lead up to that when you'd developed your telepathic talent to the point at which we could tell if you were also telekinetic."

"I would have appreciated knowing a little sooner," Alea said with irony. "How many other secrets are you hiding?"

"About my general powers, none," Gar said. "About what I can do with them, quite a few. I'll tell you about them as you develop your skills."

"I think I'd better know about them now."

"As you wish," Gar said, "but we'd better find a stream first."

They found a brook, and while he bathed Alea took out the peddler's clothing she had stored in her pack when he'd decided to disguise himself as a half-wit. She was tempted to peek while he bathed but told herself it was silly—she'd seen his whole body when he was in his idiot guise except for what the loincloth covered, and she certainly didn't want to see that! Still, the thought sent a shiver running deeply into her. She did her best to ignore its destination.

When Gar came up, amazingly clean, she turned her back to let him dress and asked, "What else can you do with these 'basic powers' of yours?"

"Heal burns, as you've seen," Gar told her. "It's telekinesis really, just moving things on a very small level—and you can perceive them with an aspect of telepathy, though you have to know what's inside the body first. Also, it's good for making explosions or stopping them, changing the nature of a substance—say, lead into gold, though that sets up dangerous radiation—and for setting fires or dousing them."

"So that's how you walked through a burning village and only singed your robe!"

"Ran, actually, from one suffering person to another. I had to knock out a few soldiers in order to save the villagers, but none of them saw me coming."

"You really had time to worry about whether or not the soldiers would remember you?"

"More a matter of trying to make sure they didn't gang up on me," Gar said, "so I didn't scruple to strike from behind. Good thing, too, if we don't want a total manhunt after me."

"Would that really bother you?"

Gar cocked his head, thinking it over. "I wouldn't mind it a bit, if we could persuade a few hundred villagers to set up an ambush for Malachi and his bandits. Since we can't, though, I'd just as soon not attract too much of their attention."

"Neither would I." Alea shuddered at the thought. "Are you done dressing yet?"

"Yes," Gar said. "Good thought about the peddler's clothing—we must be far enough away from Malachi's camp so that I won't be recognized now. Thanks."

"You're welcome." Alea turned to face him. "Let's go to town."

They followed the road down to a broad river; the town had grown up where two streams joined with a road, and people unloaded barges into wagons and vice versa. They wandered through the streets for an hour or more amid the familiar bustle of a busy trade town—apprentices wheeling loads on barrows, teamsters driving loaded wagons, merchants haggling happily and loudly. No one seemed to take any particular notice of them; what was another peddler more or less in this busy place?

They found a market where people traded rutabagas for iron ingots, wool for cloth, and amber for spices. There were inns, frequented by merchants and farmers, where guests paid with anything from ounces of metal to piglets on the hoof. They found streets filled with craftsmen—blacksmiths and silversmiths and carpenters and tradesmen of all kinds who would accept almost any kind of goods for their services.

They didn't find a government.

When they stopped for lunch at a food stall in a small park, Alea had to fight valiantly to keep from saying, "I told you so." Instead, she offered, "That street with tradesmen—the blacksmith did seem to be some kind of leader."

"Yes, the other people deferred to his opinion, and that one man did come to discuss the problem with his son," Gar agreed, "but that's a far cry from actually giving orders and making sure they're obeyed."

"Does a government *have* to compel people?" Alea asked.

"If it doesn't, it's just a debating society."

Alea thought that one over for a minute, then asked, "What if a debating society decides what people should do and comes with their fists if anybody refuses?"

"That's a government," Gar admitted.

"Then we've seen that happening in every village we've visited. It just hasn't been formal and official."

"Yes, neighbors deciding what everyone in the village should do about a given situation," Gar agreed. "They use disapproval and the silent treatment instead of fists, but that's enough enforcement for me to be willing to call it a form of government."

"Then why are you still looking?"

"Because it's only happening village by village," Gar explained. "Who coordinates all the villages? Who makes sure there's a full warehouse in case there's a bad harvest? Who patrols the roadway to guard against bandits? Nobody!"

"But every village has a granary," Alea retorted, "and the people seem to have survived the lean years." Her lips tightened at the memory of the youth village. "I admit it would be very nice to have someone put down General Malachi and his bandits—but everyone seems to be sure the Scarlet Company will take care of him."

"I don't call a band of assassins a government," Gar grunted. "Mind you, the history books do tell about some assassin bosses who have become warlords, then eventually kings, but no one has ever mentioned the Scarlet Company doing any such thing."

"At least the local chapter here should be well funded," Alea said. "I've seen a collection box in every plaza."

"How do they manage the collecting?" Gar wondered. "Do

the boxes have hollow posts emptying into a network of underground tunnels?"

"I think everyone's afraid to look and even more afraid to tell," Alea said. "Besides, emptying the boxes at two o'clock in the morning would give you quite a bit of privacy."

"The members of the Scarlet Company would have to be very devoted to get up in the middle of every night." Gar frowned. "Unless they were awake at that time anyway."

"Who would be conscious at two o'clock in the morning?" Alea protested.

"Priests and priestesses in a round-the-clock vigil." Gar stood and took up his staff again. "Let's go find a temple."

He chose the biggest temple, of course, which was really a toss-up—there were two the same size at the top of the hill around which the town had grown. The locals not having coins, he tossed a shoe; it landed sole-up, so he went into the left-hand temple. Alea sighed with martyred patience and followed.

The interior was a cavern, its roof soaring up above a line of small windows into shadow. At the far side, a twenty-foot-tall statue of a man sat in an ornate marble chair. His face was handsome, grave, and kindly beneath a well-trimmed jawline beard. He wore draped robes and held a curious scepter topped by an onion-shaped bulb with an elongated point. He was old enough to be a father but young enough to be a lover.

"So this is the god." Gar stood frowning up, as though measuring himself against the statue.

"I suppose men have to have something to pray to, just as women do," Alea said, somewhat waspishly, "since they're lacking in imagination."

"Not lacking in memory, though." Gar pointed at the scepter. "That's a lightning rod."

Alea stared, then recognized the shape from the entry on Herkimer's screen.

"Other gods throw lightning," Gar said. "This one diverts it, shields you from it. He's a protector."

"Protectors can become tyrants," Alea said.

"Not here, it seems." Gar rested his chin on his folded hands atop his staff and gazed up at the statue, brooding. "He doesn't hold a shield, either—he's prepared to protect his people from natural disasters, not from one another."

Then he'd better learn, Alea thought, but said instead, "Perhaps he leaves that to the goddess."

"You mean the priestesses might lead the Scarlet Company?" Gar turned to frown at her. "A good thought. How can we test it?"

Alea stared back at him, caught flat-footed but thinking fast. "Find a priest," she said. "You ask him questions—I'll listen to what he doesn't say."

"Fair enough." Gar looked up as a middle-aged man in the robes of a priest came out from behind the statue. He saw the companions and came toward them with a gentle, encouraging smile. "There is no ceremony here until evening, friends. Have you come because you are troubled in your hearts?"

"In my mind, rather, Reverend," Gar said.

"Ah." The priest nodded, still smiling, and gestured toward a small door at the side of the temple. "Come to a talking room, then, my friends."

He turned away, not waiting for a response. Gar exchanged a glance with Alea, then shrugged and followed the priest. Alea went along, a little surprised that she was allowed to do so—at home, Odin's priests would never have allowed a woman to set foot in his temple, let alone an inner chamber.

The room was perhaps eight feet by ten, the longer walls curving with the shape of the temple, whitewashed and hung with tapestries showing the god in his chariot, riding through a storm with lightning being sucked into his scepter. Another showed the temple with the sun rising behind it, and inside the sun the god in his chariot. A third showed a huge tree, its trunk in the shape of the god. Alea caught her breath; in this one form, the priests summed up three of Midgard's gods.

The priest gestured to two hourglass-shaped chairs and sat in another across from them; at his side was a small table with a tall pitcher and two cups. "I must know first if this is a matter of the heart, for if it is, we should go to the goddess's temple and ask a priestess to join us. Are you bonded, my friends? Or considering bonding?"

Not "son" or "daughter," Alea noted—just "friends." "No, Reverend," she said, "we are only fellow travelers, road companions." She felt a churning within her, the sort of apprehension that goes with speaking a lie, but pushed it out of her mind.

"It is wise not to travel alone, either on the roads or in life," the priest acknowledged. "What troubles you, then, my friends?"

"The sages, Reverend," Gar replied, and at the priest's puzzled look, explained, "We're from very far away, very far indeed, and have no such wise men where we come from."

"I see," the priest said slowly. "But what could trouble you about good and gentle people who only lead others into wisdom?"

"The ease with which they advise," Gar said carefully, "and the people's quickness to turn to them when they are in difficulty. You approve of them, then?"

"Approve?" the priest asked in astonishment. "It is not something for approval or disapproval—the sages simply *are*."

"A force of nature?" Gar asked. "Still, when people are troubled, should they not come to a priest or priestess instead of to a sage?"

"Ah, I see your problem." The priest's face smoothed into a smile. "The great crises in their lives they bring to us, the emotional turmoil that knots them up so that they cannot go on with living—but lesser problems they take to their sages, and glad we are to have them do so."

"The sages relieve you of some of the burden, then," Gar said slowly.

"There is that," the priest acknowledged, "but it is more. We are priests; our concern is religion—worship of the god and goddess, and the ways in which the soul relates to them."

"Not morality?" Gar frowned.

"A moral life is a continuing prayer," the priest explained. "The sages, however, seek to understand all the other ways in which people should relate to the world, and to one another."

Gar still frowned. "Surely they have some concern for the soul!"

"Surely they do," the priest agreed, "and perhaps of a greater soul, a union of all souls—but only there do we begin to share concerns."

"You are not jealous, then?" Gar asked. "You do not see them as rivals?"

The priest laughed gently. "Rivals? Oh no, my friend! We are not jealous at all, for we see the god and goddess as containing all souls that strive to do right, whereas the sages see that all souls unite to form a god."

"You are content with this division?" Gar's voice was carefully neutral.

"Quite content, for their wisdom differs from ours, and the people bring their everyday problems to the sages, but their eternal problems to us."

"I see . . . I think," Gar said. He gave Alea a perplexed glance, but she could only lift her shoulders in a tiny shrug. He turned back to the priest. "So the sages are not religious, only philosophers and counselors?"

"Counselors, yes—though rather cryptic ones." The priest's smile was amused.

"I see," Gar said slowly. "In that case, Reverend, I have only one question left."

"Ask, my friend."

"Who empties the Scarlet Company's collection boxes?"

14

The priest blinked with surprise at the change of topic but answered easily. "The god knows, my friend, and the goddess—but no one else, except the Scarlet Company itself."

"And if anyone else knows, they're not telling," Gar said in an angry undertone as he strode down the temple steps.

Alea hurried to catch up with him. "He really doesn't know, Gar. His mind was blank with astonishment and no knowledge of the answer filled it."

"I didn't detect anything else," Gar agreed, "and it was an ambush question, sprung on him out of nowhere. If he knew the answer, it would have leaped to mind immediately, no matter how well he kept it from showing in his face."

"Perhaps there really is no one who knows about the Scarlet Company—except the few who are in it."

"And they do seem to be very few," Gar agreed, "a minor element in daily life, always there at the back of people's minds but rarely thought of—they really don't have much to do with day-to-day living." He halted, fists clenching on his staff and driving its heel against the stone step. "Blast! It's all wrong, all completely wrong! It just can't happen this way!"

Alea hid a smile.

"A society can't exist without a government," Gar ranted, "not even a village culture like this one! There has to be a ruler, a council of councils, an Allthing, a Parliament, a committee of the wealthy and powerful, a hierarchy of priests—something!"

"We've looked everywhere," Alea demurred.

"There must be someplace we've missed, some structure we haven't thought of! Peace and prosperity are impossible without government, even if all it does is keep people from robbing one another and killing each other off!"

"The villagers themselves do that, in the countryside," Alea reminded him, "and the neighborhoods seem to do the same in this town. When everybody knows everybody else's business, you can't get away with anything."

"So all they have to do is gang up on the culprit and scold him into unbearable humiliation until he straightens out—and if he won't straighten, they kick him out to live in the forests as well as he can!"

"Where he becomes a bandit," Alea said, "but there aren't enough of them to be much of a threat until somebody like General Malachi comes along."

"Whereupon they all sit back and wait for the Scarlet Company to stop him," Gar fumed. "Don't the idiots realize that they have to band together, train for battle, elect a war leader, do *something* to stop him themselves?"

Alea said nothing, only fought to keep a straight face.

"They don't, and they never will!" Gar growled. "Come on, let's get out of this town—so much innocence is oppressive! Let's go out into the countryside, where wild animals fight it out and the only order is the food chain!"

"Good idea," Alea said, "but I'd rather not be in the middle of that food chain."

"No, the top is a much better place," Gar said, frowning, "and right now, that looks to be General Malachi and his band."

"I don't want to be gobbled up by them, either!"

"Definitely not to my taste," Gar agreed. "I'd better become a half-wit again. Let's go, Alea. One more good look around, say five more villages, and I just might have to give up in defeat and admit there's a planet that doesn't need me!"

Alea swallowed her amusement and kept pace with him to the city limits.

As soon as they were out of sight of the town, they stepped into a thicket, where Gar stripped off his trader's clothes and folded them. Alea packed them away as Gar rubbed dirt on assorted portions of his anatomy and gave his face a light powdering of grime. Then, wearing only a loincloth and a blanket, he followed Alea out onto the road. As she strode west, Gar hunched, scuttling beside her, and said, "It's odd,—although I think it's very important to be honest with my friends, I don't hesitate for a second to put on a deception like this for my enemies."

"That's nothing strange," Alea said scornfully. "You might as well say that a warrior in battle can't hit his enemies unless he's willing to hit his friends, too."

"Well, that's so," Gar said thoughtfully. "I'd always thought of honesty as a moral issue, not a tactical one."

"Honesty isn't. Dishonesty is," Alea told him. "Besides, anyone believing you're a half-wit is doing their own deceiving. A blind man could tell you're no idiot."

"Why, thank you," Gar said, somewhat surprised. "Still, it's the ones with keen eyesight I'm worried about, not the blind."

"If you feel any guilt, it should be for the idiots," Alea snapped. "That's whom you're insulting with that disguise."

"Well, yes," Gar said, "but then, I *am* an idiot compared to some men I've heard of."

And to some women who've heard you, Alea thought waspishly. In the same tone, she said, "Don't let that worry you. All men are fools in one way or another."

"And all women are wise?" Gar asked.

"If I want a wise woman, there are plenty of them in the forest," Alea retorted, "though I'm not one to hold with potions and simples."

"Present company excepted, of course?"

"You may not notice half the things you should," Alea said, "but that doesn't make you simple. You do a good job of faking, though."

"How do you know I'm not really doing a good job of pretending not to notice?"

That gave Alea pause—but not a long one. "Because you said you value honesty with your friends."

"Yes, but you have to weigh one good action against another," Gar said. "It's all right to lie about small things to keep from hurting someone's feelings."

Alea stopped, rounding on him. "You mean you see a host of flaws in me you don't talk about!"

"Not flaws," Gar said, "but traits that you might think are flaws."

"Such as?" Alea snapped.

"Taking every chance you can to pick an argument with me," Gar said.

"I do not!"

"You see?" Gar asked. "It's only a matter of my perceptions, and I'm likely enough to be wrong—so if I did think you were quarrelsome, it wouldn't be right to say so."

"I'm not quarrelsome!"

"Perhaps not, but you do enjoy a good argument." Gar's eyes were alight with the pleasure of this one.

"Oh, and I'm the only one, am I?" Alea's eyes were gleaming, too. She felt angered and aggravated but felt a strange sort of relaxation, too—as though she knew no harm could come from this.

She was wrong. The two were so intent on their wrangling that they forgot to pay attention to the thoughts around them, and the patrol came upon them before they knew it.

The sound of hoofbeats and the shouts to halt finally penetrated. Alea spun with a gasp, staring at the approaching horsemen.

"Run!" Gar snapped. "I'll keep them from following until you're good and lost!"

"I can't leave you to fight them alone!" Alea's staff snapped up to guard.

"Of course you can! They won't hurt me, though I'll let them think they have! And how will I break free of them if you aren't there to shoot an arrow at the right moment? Run—please!"

"Oh, all right!" Alea huffed as she turned and dove into the roadside underbrush.

Men shouted behind her, and trotting hooves broke into a gallop. Gar roared, and Alea risked a look back. Through the screen of leaves, she saw the "half-wit" unfold into a grizzly bear, charging the leader's horse. The beast reared, screaming with fright, and the bandit, taken by surprise, went sprawling with a bellow of pain. Gar leaped, caught the reins left-handed and hung on, dragging the horse down, then vaulting onto its back, staff still in his right hand.

The leader bellowed with anger as he scrambled to his feet, shouting, "To me! Seize this impudent idiot!"

The two men who had been chasing Alea reined in, turned their horses, and went galloping back. The other three closed on Gar, pulling clubs from their belts and swinging.

They landed on shoulder and ribs. Gar howled with pain, swinging his staff in wild overhand arcs. They seemed to be the flailings of an untrained, uncoordinated simpleton, but Alea heard more knocks on wood than thuds on flesh—and knew that the blows that did land on Gar didn't do anywhere nearly as much harm as they seemed to, that he had robbed them of their force with telekinesis. Still, he roared in agony and she winced, knowing that he would be black and blue tomorrow. *All right, I'm safe!* she thought.

Gar promptly fell off the horse and cowered in the roadway, wailing, arms up to protect his head and face. Clubs drubbed on his back until the red-faced leader held up a hand and called, "Enough!"

His men held off but still hovered near, clubs raised. The leader stepped up to seize Gar's hair and yank his head back. "Let that be a lesson to you, bucko, and don't you ever raise your hand to a sergeant or an officer again! From now on you'll do as you're told, and right quickly, too—for you're one of General Malachi's soldiers now!"

"Him? A soldier?" one of the bandits cried, scandalized.

"And why not, I'd like to know?" the sergeant demanded. "He's big, and scary when he's angry, we've all seen that—and he can fight, though not very well. He'll do fine to drive in front of us against the next batch of villagers who decide to talk back to General Malachi."

"Drive?" Gar asked, peeking through his fingers.

"That's right, drive, like the ox you are!" the sergeant snapped. He turned to his men. "Tie his hands with a leading rope and let him run behind my horse."

"Aye, Sergeant!" one of the men said, gloating. "We can drive him against the enemy broken as well as whole!"

"He'll have to be able to walk, at least," the sergeant grunted. "If he falls, we'll give him a chance to get up—but he'll be properly weary before he gets back to camp!"

As they lashed his hands together, Gar thought, *Don't worry, Alea—they won't do me any real damage, no matter how badly they want to. Besides, after what we've seen, I'm all ready to meet General Malachi again!*

Alea shuddered at the thought. *He may have been right when he thought you were a danger to him—but don't forget he's a danger to you, too! I want you back alive, Gar Pike, not in pieces!*

His answer wasn't worded, only a warm glow that seemed to enfold her for a second, then withdrew as the sergeant kicked his horse into a trot and Gar jerked forward as the rope tightened. Then he was off running, chasing the tail of a cavalry horse while the other bandits whooped and rode alongside, aiming stinging slaps at his head and shoulders. Gar wailed dolefully and stumbled rather theatrically, but managed to keep up.

Alea stood watching him go, numbed and shaken. Why had he answered her scolding with such warmth? What did he think she'd meant, anyway?

And was he right?

Unnerved, she stared after the soldiers until they were gone. Then she realized that she had been staring at an empty road for several minutes and gave herself an impatient shake. She knew what to do, what she had done before—the physical part of it, at least.

She found a tree with low branches, took a rope from her pack and tied it to the straps, also her staff, then laid them on the ground and leaped up to sit on the lowest limb. She rose to her feet and started climbing. Twenty feet high, she found a branch that forked almost at the trunk and sat down, tieing herself to the trunk with the end of the rope. Then she hauled up her gear to set the pack on the fork before her and her staff across her knees. There, where she would be secure from attack for at least long enough to come awake and defend herself should the need arise, she closed her eyes, listening for Gar's thoughts, concentrating on them until they became more real than the breeze that fanned her cheek or the songs of the birds that began to come back and settle near her, thinking the immobile woman only part of the tree.

Gar came panting into the camp, stumbling behind the sergeant's horse, and this time he wasn't faking. The sergeant reined in and Gar fell to his knees, sucking air in hoarse gasps and shivering in the chill autumn air. Inside, though, he was simmering with anger at the casual cruelty of his captors and ready to explode with frustration at a country in which everything progressed smoothly and peacefully, but without a government.

Everything, that is, except the bandits and a baby warlord named General Malachi who was showing signs of growing up all too fast—into a full-fledged tyrant. Gar might not have been able to find the government or even the Scarlet Company that was not stopping General Malachi, but he could certainly do it himself.

No! Alea thought with anguish. *They'll kill you!*

But Gar wasn't listening—he was looking up in feigned fear and apprehension at the sergeant, who was sneering, "Aye, you should cower! If General Malachi were here, he'd see you scourged smartly, be sure! But he's not and not likely to be, for we're an outpost, here to watch our next target, spy out its supply routes, and be ready to fall upon it when the general brings up his main force."

Gar felt a stab of keen disappointment and an urge to break out of this nest of robbers, to hike back along the highway until he found the main camp and a general he could strangle. Still, where there was even an outpost of the army, the general would come sooner or later, and before he did, Gar might be able to size up the situation and learn its weak points. With telekinesis and teleportation, he probably could have killed Malachi by a bearlike rush, main force, and a straightforward attack, but the chances of his coming away alive weren't as high as he would have liked. He throttled down his impatience and his anger, deciding to stay, learn the lay of the land, and be waiting to ambush the general when he came.

The sergeant stepped back, surveying Gar as though judging his worth. "Filthy beggar, aren't you? Wash him, boys."

Gar yelped as the soldiers descended on him, two to each arm and leg, and hauled him running to the nearest horse trough. They slung him in; then six of them held him down while the other two scrubbed with harsh soap and the sort of brush that's used on horses. The sergeant stood by, grinning and calling directions.

"Don't forget his hair, there's liable to be as many lice in there as there are squirrels in the wood! Under his armpits, now, that's the way! And don't forget to reach where he can't, or likely doesn't."

Gar howled, and didn't have to pretend—the stiff brush was scraping him raw.

Finally the sergeant called, "That should do him, now. Haul him out and see if he's improved."

The soldiers yanked and Gar came out of the tub, lurching forward until he saw the spear point aimed at his chest and froze. He was pink and glowing with the scrubbing; he felt as though there couldn't be a patch of skin left on his whole body.

Then a cold breeze blew and he began to shiver.

The sergeant threw him a length of rough cloth that would have made burlap look fine. "Rub yourself down with that. Boys, fetch him our largest uniform."

Uniform? Looking out over the camp, Gar saw that all the men were indeed wearing brown tunics and tan leggins. They were lounging around a broad clearing a hundred feet across, a natural tableland that supported only a few trees, enough to give cover to sixty tents and the men who lived in them. The fires were low and smokeless, the ground trodden bare. Here and there, a man was chopping wood or hauling water, but most were sharpening their weapons or currying their horses.

Cloth struck Gar in the face.

"There, that's the largest we've got," the sergeant said. "It will have to do. Help him into it, boys."

The soldiers cheered with the fun of another game. Gar squawked as they descended on him, yanking the tunic down over his head; he heard something rip. They knocked him down to pull the leggins up and lash them in place with black cross garters. Gar started to fight, then caught himself and throttled it down to only enough to convince them he was a terrified, uncoordinated idiot.

Finally they hauled him upright and yanked the cowl of his tunic up to cover his head.

"There you are, Sergeant," one of them said, thumping Gar

on the chest as he turned to his boss. "As smart a soldier as you've ever seen."

The sergeant looked and brayed laughter.

Gar could imagine why. The sleeves of the tunic seemed as tight as tourniquets; their cuffs ended three inches below his elbows. The seams at the shoulders had split, leaving several inches of bare skin, and the only reason the leggins weren't cutting off his circulation was because they had been sewn to be twice as wide as a man would need, depending on the cross garters to make them fit. Gar wore the cross garters because his "fellow" soldiers had tied them on, not because he needed them. The leggins ended halfway down his shins, of course, and they'd had to cut off the ends of the buskins, leaving his toes sticking out. *At least, when General Malachi sees me, he won't recognize me.*

"Well, you'll do, I suppose," the sergeant said. "Come on now, and I'll show you the quarry we're set to watch."

He led Gar over to the edge of the plateau, the other soldiers trooping along around him with raucous comments.

"Down there." The sergeant pointed.

Gar looked down where the hillside fell away, the tops of the trees dropping in steps, letting him clearly see the shining curves of the river below, the tawny line of the road that intersected it, and where they joined, the sprawl of the town in which he had slept the night past.

They put him to work hauling water to the kitchen and timbers to the men who were setting up a wooden wall. After dinner, though, Gar had a few minutes to himself. He gazed off into space with vacant eyes, which no one would think unusual in a half-wit, but his mind was engaged in a lively discussion.

Don't worry about me, Alea—I'm in no danger, worse luck.

Why not? Alea asked, but couldn't keep the message free of her feelings of relief.

Thanks for caring, Gar answered, his thoughts colored by the warmth of affection. *Apparently General Malachi isn't going to be here for some time, if at all—this is just an outpost, a handful of troops here to scout the lay of the land and the best routes for invasion. Until Malachi does come, no one's apt to recognize me—especially not in their own uniform, if you can call this outfit that.*

Don't sound so disappointed, Alea thought. *If the chief bully isn't coming, why are you bothering to stay?*

Because this is an excellent place to learn his plans, Gar answered, *and when I know their invasion tactics, I can warn the town and tell them how to defend themselves. They could do what these bandits are doing, for starters—build themselves a wall of sharpened timbers.*

Then I'll go tell them so! Alea thought. *At the very least, I can tell them they're in danger.*

A good thought, Gar said slowly, *but if General Malachi has agents in the town, you could be in danger.*

I accepted danger when I landed on this planet, Alea retorted. *How about you? There's a limit to how many men you can fight off by thinking at them!*

There's danger, yes, Gar thought slowly, *but I've faced much worse, and this is too good a chance to pass up—studying the enemy on his home ground.*

Alea caught the overtones to his thoughts, and frowned. *There's more to it than that, isn't there? You're still hoping to find a government!*

No, I've given up on that, Gar answered, *but I might learn something about this band of thugs, and why such a gentle civilization could produce so many of them.*

. . .

Alea set out at first light and came back to the town in the afternoon. As she walked down the road and in among the houses, she saw what Gar meant about a wall—there was nothing to keep anyone from simply walking in, as she had, and the broad stretches of grass and patches of garden around the city were an open invitation to horsemen to enter riding, trampling vegetables and people. She remembered the charred timbers of the new village and shuddered. That could not be allowed to happen again!

She stopped the first citizen she saw by catching his shoulder. "Sir," she commanded, "defend yourself!"

15

The citizen was an old man, nearly bald, but with quick, bright eyes that took her in at a glance, weighed her, and decided to take her seriously. "Defend myself? Why? Do you mean to strike me?"

"Not only you," Alea said impatiently, "your whole town! And no, it won't be me who attacks you—it will be General Malachi with all his army!"

The man relaxed with a smile. "General Malachi? Is that all?"

"All!" Alea squawked. "Burning your houses and looting your shops? Slaughter and torture? *All*?"

The man waved away the threat. "Surely it won't come to that. The Scarlet Company will stop him before he comes near."

"Tell that to the four villages he conquered! Tell it to the smoking, charred ruin that was the hopeful beginning of a new village! Tell it to the young folk who were killed or hauled away to slave and whore for Malachi's bandits! Tell it to the young men who mean you no harm but will come charging against you with swords in their hands because they've spears at their backs!"

The citizen stared, unnerved, but collected himself and objected, "Surely you exaggerate."

"No, actually, I'm holding back the worst of it."

"It can't happen here," the man said with finality. "Perhaps in a small village full of peasants, but this is a *town.* General Malachi wouldn't even try."

"Wrong! Being a town is all the more reason for him to ride down upon you! You're wealthy, you have a huge store of riches to delight his men—and with your barges, he can ferry his army across the river and start conquering the villages there!"

"Then surely the Scarlet Company will stop him here," the man said stubbornly. "If you really think there's danger, good woman, you're perfectly free to scream it from the rooftops—but I don't think you'll find any to believe you. Good day."

He turned away and Alea nearly did scream—with exasperation.

She did, however, walk up and down every street and lane in the town, telling everyone she met, as loudly as she could, about their danger. Most of them glanced at her with frightened eyes and hurried on their way, leaving her to turn and finish her sentence to the next person before that one, too, scuttled away. Now and then she managed to back a man or woman into a corner, haranguing the person until she was finally asked, insistently and sometimes angrily, to stop spouting such nonsense.

She could have wept with frustration.

By the time sundown came and she slumped exhausted onto a bench outside an inn, she was past anger and on the verge of despair. The fools, the blind fools! They almost deserved to have General Malachi and his troops grind them into their river mud.

Almost. No one deserved that, not even self-blinded, complacent idiots.

She needed someone to listen to her rant about them—and it must be dinnertime for the troops. *Gar,* she thought, *can we talk?*

His answer was so immediate that she knew he must have been waiting for her call. *Of course, though there isn't much to tell—only the usual soldier's round of drudgery and boredom. They do have some idea of drill, though it's very rudimentary—only making us practice marching forward with spears in our backs while they shout and bellow at us and wave weapons in our faces.*

Making sure you'll be more afraid of them than of the enemy you face, Alea thought sourly.

It's working on most of the other footmen, Gar told her. *They must be captives from the villages Malachi has conquered.*

Alea's stomach sank. *Do you—do you recognize any of our teenage hosts?*

One or two, but they're so dull-eyed and cowed that I don't think they'd recognize me even if I were dressed as they last saw me—and the wide-eyed cringing simpleton I'm playing should be safe from discovery.

I certainly hope he is. Alea could easily imagine one of the young men betraying Gar in hopes of a little consideration from his captors.

What luck in the town? Gar asked.

Absolutely none, Alea thought in disgust. *These people wouldn't believe the dam had broken unless they were breathing water!*

Don't they believe the stories about General Malachi?

Oh, they believe them easily enough. In fact, everybody has heard of him—but nobody believes he'd attack anything as big as their town!

I've heard of cities deluded by their own self-importance. Gar sighed. *But this is too much. Won't a single one of them lift a spear in his own defense?*

Why bother? Alea thought bitterly. *They're convinced the Scarlet Company will protect them—bring General Malachi and his army to their knees overnight! I tell you, if their complacency has any grounds, the Scarlet Company must be a full-scale army!*

Perhaps it is, Gar thought somberly, *just very well hidden. Well, if they won't listen to you, they deserve what they get—but maybe they have a reason for their calm.*

If they do, they're certainly closemouthed about it, Alea replied. *No one's ever seen the Scarlet Company, or anyone from it—though I suppose it could be that they're so scary no one wants to even think about them.*

Well, if we can't find out what they're like now, Gar thought, *maybe we can get some idea from their history. I'll ask around and see if anyone knows . . .*

Don't you dare! Alea's thought had all the force of terror. *Your only protection is seeming to be an idiot, and simpletons don't go around asking about the past! The ones I knew back ho—back on Midgard, they didn't even know there* was *a past!*

If you say so, Gar thought doubtfully, *but we have to know whether or not there's any reason to hope that the Scarlet Company will bail them out.*

I'll ask! You just sit tight and watch! If anybody here knows anything more about the Scarlet Company than we do, I'll find out by this time tomorrow!

You don't think anyone does know about it, do you? Gar asked slowly.

I'm beginning to doubt that it exists, Alea thought grimly. *I'll ask anyway, though—tomorrow. Right now, I'd better find a safe place to sleep.*

The next morning, Alea set out to discover anyone who knew anything about the Scarlet Company. She strolled along the docks, claiming to be hunting a missing bondmate and refusing offers to take his place. She worked a mention of the Scarlet

Company into every conversation while she listened intently for the other person's thoughts but never caught anything coherent, only a passing aura of admiration and fear. She did see a great number of barges and smaller riverboats coming in, watched their owners bargain with wholesalers, then watched them unload produce and reload salt, spices, iron ingots, bars of tin and copper, and the other commodities that a farming village needed but couldn't produce for itself.

Then she made the rounds of the town limits, reasoning that travelers would have heard of the Scarlet Company, and struck up conversations where the town streets joined the main roads. She saw cart after cart coming in filled with preserved hams, barrels of salt beef and ale, furs and sheepskins and bales of wool; she saw other carts rolling out with more metal and dye and other things the villagers didn't have around them—but no one she talked to had the guilty or guarded reactions she expected of a Scarlet Company member.

In the evening, she paced from neighborhood to neighborhood, seeing the people come out of their cottages to chat and play while the older citizens sat in circles and discussed earnestly whether or not a given girl should be bonded to a given boy, whether a young man who had struck another was a bully and should be exiled, working out a schedule for their neighbors to haul away garbage, even listening to an argument between two women as to whether or not the first woman had the right to milk the other's cow if it wandered into her yard (they decided that the two should barter for the milk and build a stout fence). Wherever she could, Alea mentioned the Scarlet Company, but her mind caught only the usual awe, and sometimes relief that the Scarlet Company was there to stop bullies.

Finally, as darkness fell, she traded a bit of copper for a bed in the single-women's room at an inn, chatted with her neighbors and managed to mention the Scarlet Company, but received only the usual answers, then politely excused herself for her evening "meditations." The other women stared at her in surprise, then quickly said "Of course" and left her alone.

Alea felt a moment of surprise of her own, at their obvious awe—even if it was rare for a person to meditate before sleeping, surely it wasn't anything remarkable—then settled herself, let the cares of the day drift through her mind, slow, and settle, then thought, *Gar.*

Here. Gar's thoughts were unutterably weary.

Alea's mind moved to a higher level of alertness. *What has happened?*

Nothing, Gar thought, *but it could have.* Then he remembered the key incident of the day, letting her share it with him.

The recruits had come marching into camp at daybreak—or trying to march, anyway; they hadn't quite caught the knack of stepping in unison, and the broken branches they were carrying in lieu of spears lay at all different angles across their chests. Nonetheless, they were at least trying to look military. When their leader called, "Halt!" they all stamped as they stopped.

So did Gar's heart, almost. He recognized the hard-faced leader—Crel, one of the few free survivors of the young people's village. When he had first seen the lad, his face had glowed with health, happiness, and the pleasure of the company of his youthful friends. He had been smiling, easygoing, and genial. Now, though, he was gaunt, steely-eyed, and tense.

The lieutenant came forward grinning. "Very good, very good—for men who haven't been taught a thing. So you want to join General Malachi's army, do you?"

"We do!" the men chorused, turning to him.

"Keep your eyes front!" the lieutenant snapped.

They jumped and whipped their gazes back to the hair of the men ahead of them.

"Shoulders straight! Bellies in! Hold those spears straight up, if you can remember which end you think has the tip!" The lieutenant prowled along the line. "You're filthy, you stink, your clothes are ragged! You all need your hair cropped to your skulls! You're undisciplined—you need kicking into line!" He paused at the front, grinning at the leader. "Still want to join?"

"Yes!" Crel spat, and the others echoed him.

The lieutenant nodded and started to stroll around them again. "Well, you might do at that. All right, off to the barracks with you. Sergeant Chester!"

"Sir!" A sergeant came running, snapped to attention, and saluted more crisply than Gar had noticed in a day and night at the camp.

"Take these men in charge," the lieutenant commanded. "See them scoured, shorn, and uniformed. Burn those rags they're wearing, then set them to their tasks."

"Yes, Sir!" Sergeant Chester turned to face the recruits. " 'Ten-*shun!* No, not like that—suck those bellies in! Drop those sticks, they'll do for the fire. Thumbs along the seams of your leggins! Square those shoulders, don't pull 'em back! All right, now, march!"

They followed him toward the tents. Too late, Gar realized he was in their line of march and started to turn away—but Crel saw him. His eyes widened with the shock of recognition and Gar could hear his thought: *Was he a spy for the bandits all along?* Then Gar's pitiful stance must have registered, because he thought, *No, the poor man's a captive and a slave.* Then he marched on and Gar breathed a sigh of relief.

He wasn't about to rely on the boy's first reaction, though—he might change his mind when he thought it over. Gar watched and, when the lad went to the latrine, Gar went after him.

Crel looked considerably better for a wash, a shave, and clean clothes, but the harshness and bitterness were still there in his face. He glanced up as Gar came in—then stared and braced himself for a fight.

"Easy, easy," Gar said softly, hoping no one would hear through the canvas walls. "I'm just the village idiot out to visit the necessary room. You don't have to have that much intelligence to know how to use a privy."

"Idiot!" Crel hissed. "Is that what they think you are?"

"I've been very careful to make sure they think so," Gar said.

"Then it was your father who came to our village." Crel's eyes filled at mention of the happy, hopeful pair of longhouses.

"No, that was me," Gar told him. "I angered General Malachi in my proper form and he set patrols to find me. I disguised myself as an old man, and they rode right by me."

"Then why disguise yourself as an idiot?"

"Because they had begun to be suspicious of the old me. The idiot was a bad choice, though—brains don't matter in a human shield, and they're quite happy to have a bear like me to prod ahead of them onto the pitchforks of the enemy—should any of them think to try to fight back. I'd rather not disillusion them." He let that sink in for a few seconds, then added. "I gather you'd just as soon they didn't find out which village you came from, either."

"That's right enough," the lad said slowly. "Are you making a deal?"

"Only pointing out our mutual interest," Gar said, "that neither of us wants his real nature bandied about."

"So you won't tell them where I come from if I don't tell what you really are," Crel said slowly. "Before I agree to that, though, I'd like to know why you're here."

"Because I was caught," Gar said simply. "I'm trying to figure out a way to stay alive when they attack that town down below us and drive me ahead with the other slaves, to draw whatever kind of weapons the town men have. So far I'm ahead of the game—none of them are going to expect me to try something clever at the last minute. What are you here for?"

"Why is everyone?" Crel asked bitterly. "I want to be on the winning side."

Gar stared at him for a moment, wondering whether Crel intended to be with the winners, or for his side to win because he was on it. Then he nodded. "Deal?"

"Deal," Crel said.

I can't believe he'd betray the memory of his friends like that! Alea thought.

Neither can I, but it's not for me to lecture him after what he's been through, Gar replied. *What about your day? Find anything worth knowing?*

Nothing, except that everyone's so sure of the Scarlet Company that they don't even bother thinking about it. Alea's thoughts simmered with frustration. *Of course, when I did put the thought into their minds, it scared them. They pushed it away as quickly as they could.*

Sure of the Scarlet Company but afraid of it too, Gar mused. *How about the town in general?*

No government, if that's what you mean, Alea thought wearily. *I learned there's a great deal of commerce. Barges and carts are coming and going all the time, constantly being loaded and unloaded, if that matters to you.*

Actually, it does, Gar thought slowly.

Alea stiffened, catching the complex of associations that came with the words—an image of a web with the town at its center, every strand vibrating with the necessities of life. *I see,* she thought slowly. *The town controls the villages even without a government.*

Only by being the central market, Gar thought, *but there are many villages and only the one town. If the merchants decided to stop dealing with one of them, that village would suffer harshly, maybe even die if it had a year of bad crops and no way to bring food from other villages.*

But the merchants wouldn't do that! Alea thought.

No, they wouldn't, came the slow answer, *but they are managing the market, which means they're controlling the economies of the villages.*

Have you found your government at last? Alea thought acidly.

No, Gar replied, still slowly, *but I'm beginning to understand how they can manage without one. Of course,* he added hastily, *it only works as long as the town doesn't grow too greedy.*

I suppose the priestesses take care of that, Alea mused, *the priestesses and the sages.*

Yes. Gar seemed to be brooding. *This looks to be one area in which the Scarlet Company would not be watching for bullies.*

But she caught the thought he didn't mean to send—that an economic bully was still a bully, and the Scarlet Company might have an interest after all.

So the next day, she went to talk to the people who presumably kept the merchants from being bullies—though as she walked up the steps of the goddess's temple, she couldn't help but think that the priestesses certainly wouldn't be paying much attention to economic systems.

She entered the cool domed area and stood facing the statue of the goddess in her aspect as mother. There were no seats, so she was still standing half an hour later when a priestess came in and found her brooding over the resemblance between Freya and this mother-goddess.

The priestess approached with a keen gaze. Apparently deciding that Alea was praying, she stood at a discreet distance and waited until Alea turned with a little frown, then stared at the woman.

"Do you come only to pray," the priestess asked gently, "or do you need to talk with me?"

"I wish to become a priestess," Alea answered, "or at least, to learn if I have the gift of piety."

The woman gazed at her, a careful, brooding look, then smiled and said, "There is more to it than piety, but you may have the gift for it indeed. Come, let us talk to the High Priestess."

That evening, when Alea sat down and relaxed into meditation, she was able to tell Gar, *I am a novice priestess now.*

She wasn't prepared for the panic and horror behind his thoughts as he protested. Dazed, she leaned into the fury of the blast and, as it began to slacken, caught beneath it the fear that she would be trapped on this benighted planet and that, moreover, he would be denied her company. Touched, she smiled and thought, *Don't worry, companion. I'm not serious about it—only hoping to learn anything they may know about the Scarlet Company.*

Oh. Well, that's reassuring. Gar calmed considerably. *No one has mentioned anything yet, I take it?*

No, but I have learned that they have a library. They shouldn't mind an illiterate peasant leafing through the books to look at the pictures.

Now Gar's tone was amused. *If they're careless enough to let you in, they deserve what they get. Let me know if the plot's any good.*

The next day, Alea went to the priestess who had inducted her into the temple and asked, with some anxiety, "Lady, you said that there was more needed of me than piety."

The priestess nodded gravely. "A great deal more."

"May I ask what?"

"Fortitude, and the willingness to sacrifice comforts and luxuries."

"I am truly willing! As to fortitude, try me!"

"So we shall," the priestess murmured. "So we do. Have you the patience to wait until we tell you that you have passed the test?"

Alea bowed her head, abashed. "I have never had overly much patience."

"That we shall try sorely," the priestess promised. "However, we of the goddess may be devoted to her above all, but we express that devotion in our care of the people. Have you compassion and the desire to heal and nurture?"

"I—I think I have," Alea said hesitantly, "but older women have told me you never know until you have someone to care for."

The priestess positively beamed, pleased with Alea's humility—or realism. "It is so. Be sure that you will have ample opportunity to test those qualities."

"Are we . . . are we to protect as the Scarlet Company does?" Alea ventured.

The priestess frowned, disturbed by the question. "The Scarlet Company has nothing to do with the temples, child—or if it does, we have no knowledge of it!"

Alea sighed with relief—to cover her disappointment.

"Why would you think we did?" the priestess pressed.

"Because I thought . . . I had heard . . . Well, the priests and priestesses remind us time and again that we must treat each other with respect and kindness and be careful not to become bullies in any way!"

"Ah. Yes, that much we do." The priestess's face smoothed. "But that is not doing the Scarlet Company's work, child—it is simply giving it that much less to do."

After that interview, Alea decided that she might learn a great deal from the priestesses, but none of it would be what she wished to know at the moment. Nonetheless, she didn't resist at all when her mentor called her to assist as she made her rounds.

Her rounds, it seemed, were in one of the poorest parts of the town. The woman strolled down the streets with a basket of food and medicines on her arm, stopping to chat with everyone who wished, going in wherever she was asked to visit someone who was ill. Most were previous patients; she only had to make sure they were still mending or, if they were not, to give the patient a new medicine. Some were new, and here she was careful to explain to Alea every step of her diagnosis and treatment. Alea listened, clinging to every word; most of it she knew already, but the one or two ideas or remedies that were new to her were well worth the time.

As they went back to the temple, she frowned, lost in thought. Finally the priestess asked gently, "What troubles you, my child?"

"I see that I have a very great deal to learn, Reverend Lady," Alea answered. "May I look in the books in the library? Can I learn faster that way?"

Again the priestess virtually beamed. "Surely you can, once you learn to read—but you may go there this evening and at least look at the books."

Alea caught the thought that the woman didn't say—that if the novice really had the interest in learning that a priestess needed, turning pages to look at undecipherable scratchings and glorious pictures would turn her interest into a ravenous hunger.

So after dinner that night, she went down to the library and walked along the shelves, taking in the kind and amount of knowledge stored there. She stopped at the history section, took out a huge volume entitled *History of the World,* and took it to a reading stand, hoping the world in question would be this one. She turned the pages, realized they were of parchment and that every single character had been drawn by hand, and was staggered by the thought of the number of hours of work this library represented.

Then she turned a page and lost all thought of copyists working by candlelight as she discovered the ancestors' own view of how and why they had colonized this planet.

16

You persuaded them to let you go into the library already? Gar thought, amazed.

Oh, they're all in favor of people learning to read, Alea told him. *They just didn't know that I already could, thanks to Herkimer and his teaching program.*

They use our alphabet, then?

Our alphabet, and our language, Alea confirmed. *In fact, the writings are Terran Standard, much closer to your speech than to their descendants'.*

At least they left a record, Gar thought. *What were they trying to do here, anyway?*

Abolish war and exploitation, Alea told him. *They wanted to give their children and grandchildren a world of peace and prosperity in which everyone respected everyone else's rights and liberties.*

Utopia, Gar interpreted. *Well, they weren't the first to try to set up an ideal society. How did they go about it?*

By setting up a matriarchy, Alea explained. *They thought that patriarchal cultures were much more warlike and oppressive than matriarchal cultures, so that if you never let the male-governed cultures start, the world would be peaceful.*

Very idealistic, Gar said slowly. *How well did it work?*

As you've seen, Alea replied with a mental shrug. *The men have taken an equal place in the villages here, but they haven't become dictators, and they don't treat their wives as belongings.*

They don't have wives, properly speaking, Gar answered, his tone thoughtful. *I take it the founders thought that marriage was a form of exploitation?*

Yes. Here, if a woman doesn't like the way a man treats her, she can simply put him out of her house and out of her life.

And he goes back to the bachelors' house, Gar said, musing. *And the whole village will support her and her children—though of course she, like everyone else, will have to do her fair share of the work. Of course, we haven't really seen any cases of that.*

Alea bridled. *The youth villagers were busily exchanging partners!*

Yes, Gar thought, *but none of the others seemed to be managing on their own. Everyone seemed to be bonded and part of a family, except for the priests and priestesses.*

Well, of course, Alea thought. *That's natural.*

Yes, it is, Gar answered musing. *The important point is that neither spouse is locked into a partnership they don't want. Even Shuba was only asked to support his baby daughter, not forced to marry Agneli when she wasn't in love with him.*

They didn't force her to marry him, either, Alea snapped.

I wonder how long each will live without another partner? Gar's thoughts made an abrupt turn. *Why Neolithic, though? Did they believe in Rousseau's idea of the noble savage?*

They did, Alea confirmed. *I even ran into that phrase. They thought he was right in thinking that civilization corrupted people, so they set up their society in early agricultural villages and built in a custom of starting new villages instead of letting the old ones grow.*

Except for trade towns, Gar noted. *They did make sure people would be able to send food to others who needed it—and they cheated on medicine and agriculture, too.*

When technology developed to the point at which we could go back to tribal villages, Alea argued, *why shouldn't we?*

Mostly because tribes tend to make war on each other, Gar answered, *but if you've managed to set up a culture that limits battles to large-scale sporting events with only accidental deaths, why not indeed? Yes, it's a very seductive notion.*

You don't sound convinced, Alea thought darkly.

I've seen retrograde colonies before, Gar explained with a mental shrug. *Greed always disrupted the idyllic life.*

That's where the Scarlet Company comes in, Alea thought triumphantly.

What about it? Gar's interest sharpened to an intensity that almost frightened her—almost. She knew him too well by now to suspect anything other than hunger for knowledge.

The book didn't mention them by name, Alea told him, *but it did give two pages describing how it would be set up. It was supposed to be a secret society, its members recruited from ordinary people and going on to live ordinary lives. They would work under the cell system and never meet as a group unless they had to mass to fight an army.*

Each cell being three people and the leader only knowing one other person in one other cell who passed on orders?

That's right. Alea was somewhat nettled that he already knew it.

So before any one of them does anything dangerous that's likely to see him captured and interrogated, they can make sure that everybody he knows disappears, Gar thought. *Yes, I've heard of that.*

So it would seem, Alea thought dryly.

What does it say this secret society is supposed to do to prevent tyrants from conquering? Gar asked.

It doesn't, Alea confessed, *only that the secret society is to do whatever is necessary to stop any would-be conquerors and tyrants.*

Well, the Scarlet Company isn't doing too well at the moment, Gar thought in exasperation. *What's the matter? Is Malachi the first after all? Though I don't see how he could be.*

He isn't, Alea answered. *The book covered the first hundred years, and I found other books covering the rest of the history up till twenty years ago.*

How many tyrants tried and failed?

Alea hesitated a moment, then said, *Forty-two.*

Almost every ten years? Gar thought, aghast. *How did the Scarlet Company stop them?*

Assassination, Alea said grimly, then hurried on. *There were two times when the Company had to muster half its members in one place, though—once to ambush the warlord and his army in a mountain pass, throwing down rocks. A century later, they had to pick off another warlord's soldiers one by one as they marched through a huge forest.*

That must have required top-notch woodcraft, Gar thought. *How did they train so many so fast?*

Alea didn't answer, letting him work it out for himself.

They had agents among the bandits, Gar thought, thunderstruck. *A lot of agents!*

The book said something along that line, Alea admitted.

What a horrible life to condemn someone to, Gar thought slowly, *in danger of discovery and death every minute.*

People who had suffered enough might be willing to do it, Alea thought, *and according to the books, there are always some of those. Even without a warlord, the bandits cause grief.*

It seems there are always bandits, Gar replied. *Was that part of the ancestors' plan?*

They thought exile was kinder than imprisonment, Alea answered, *and were absolutely opposed to the death penalty, no matter what the crime. They did recognize, though, that there would always be a few men and women who managed to alienate everyone and would be cast out, that some might even be unhappy in their village society and decide to leave of their own free will.*

But they didn't realize that the outcasts would turn criminal?

The founders thought they would simply go off and establish villages of their own, Alea told him. *I guess they just didn't realize that the exiles would rob instead of hunting or farming.*

Instead, they've become a constant danger, Gar said grimly. *I wonder what happened to the women who went into exile?*

The books say the bandits found them, or they found the bandits, Alea's tone was bleak. *Beyond that, the entries only said the women were enslaved.*

I think we can assume the worst. So the people just live with the problem?

The chronicles do say that every now and then, when a particular gang had become too much of a menace, three or four villages would band together and give them a beating, Alea admitted. *Not capital punishment, really, but people would be killed in the fighting.*

As they were when a bandit chieftain decided to try to become king, Gar thought darkly. *Do the founders say how the Scarlet Company was supposed to stop them?*

No—only that its whole purpose was to prevent anyone from establishing a government over everyone else. They didn't say to use assassins.

Stated in those terms, eh? That the Scarlet Company isn't supposed to stop bullies or conquerors—it's to stop government?

Before they begin, Alea confirmed. *Yes.*

How, though? Gar thought, more to himself than to Alea. *If it's an army itself, where is it? How does it work? More to the point, what's to keep some power-hungry citizen from working his way up in the Scarlet Company and using it to take over? Did the founders say anything about that?*

Not that I've read, Alea answered, *but I have three more volumes to go. I'll tell you what I find tomorrow night.*

That next night, however, they would have more immediate problems to discuss.

Alea spent the next morning in the library, scanning the rest of the chronicles and reading in depth anything that looked promising. In the afternoon, she accompanied her patron on her rounds. They were called to help at a difficult birth, then with a child whose fever was very high, and finally with an old man who'd had a stroke. The priestess couldn't do much for him but to help make him comfortable and leave directions for exercizes in hopes that he would recover some use of the affected muscles. He tried to thank her but only succeeded in making a gargling sound.

Alea thought she recognized him, but couldn't have said from where. She read his thoughts, though, and told the priestess, "He thanks you for your kindness."

Her mentor stared. "Can you understand his cawings, then?"

"Barely," Alea said, "but I can make some sense out of them, yes." She turned back to the patient. "Am I wrong?"

The old man shook his head.

"Rest, then." Alea laid her hand on his head. "Enjoy what life has left for you—you've earned it."

But the old man shook his head again, gabbling, and she heard his thought: *I know when I'm dying.*

"You are surrounded by love," Alea said firmly. "You have reason to live."

Reason, but not enough life, said the old man's thoughts as he cawed. *I have watched you since you tried to warn me against General Malachi, or had friends watch you. You spent a whole day sounding an alarm to which no one listened. When you gave up that, you went to join the priestesses. Did you think to help General Malachi's victims when he conquered the town?*

Alea stared. Now she recognized him—the first person she

had warned to defend himself and his town! The stroke had come suddenly and aged him tremendously. "I try to help everyone wherever I find them."

I knew you had a good heart, the old man said and thought. *You truly wish to save the people from General Malachi, do you not?*

"Well, of course," Alea answered.

The old man caught her hand, though, and his words seemed to explode in her mind: *You are devoted to other people, but you are not yet a priestess. Leave the temple. Fill my place in the Scarlet Company.*

Alea stared at him, unable to move. Then she tried to wrest her hand away, but he held it with a death grip, mouthing the words, Say you will!

"I . . . will do as you ask," Alea said slowly, "if it will ease your passing."

Bless you. The old man let go of her hand and closed his eyes. *Talk to Kethro the Tailor. I can leave this world now.*

Don't you dare! Alea thought, but he had already fallen asleep. She freed her hand from his grip and looked up at the old man's wife and daughter through swimming eyes. "Care for him well," she advised. "Do not let him be alone for a second."

"Lady, we shall not," the daughter said, eyes round.

The priestess watched her, gaze speculative, but said nothing until they were out in the street again. There, though, she asked, "What did he say to you?"

"That he is dying." Alea caught her breath on a sob, bowing her head. "Reverend Lady, I—I cannot bear this."

"Can you not, then?" the priestess's gaze was probing but sympathetic.

"No! It will be bad enough in my life to watch a few people die—but to see it every day, perhaps several times in one day . . . I—I have not the strength."

"It is well you have learned that so soon." The priestess laid a hand on her shoulder. "You may still be devoted to the goddess, child, and may enter the temple to worship as much as you wish—but it would seem she has another role in life for you than that of priestess."

"I—I fear so," Alea said, head bowed still.

"Then go to discover how you must serve." The priestess touched Alea's forehead, lips, then breastbone as she said, "May the goddess grant you wisdom, kind words for all you meet, and a tender heart." She withdrew her hand with a gentle smile. "Live well, my child, and happily. Farewell."

"Farewell," Alea whispered as the other woman turned away. Alea watched her go and wondered whether she was sad or relieved to be so easily out of her new career.

She was sure, though, that she had done it well.

Head still bowed, she turned away—to seek out the booth of Kethro the Tailor.

When she sat down to meditate in the common room of an inn that night, though, she wasn't at all sure whether or not to tell Gar what had happened. Kethro had been very insistent about secrecy.

She need not have worried. As soon as she made contact with him, the problem was solved. Gar was tense as a fiddle string.

What happened? Alea demanded, appalled.

For answer, Gar's memories of the day flooded her mind.

The rider burst out of the woods, following the deer track, and slewed to a halt in the center of the camp, waving and shouting, "Attention! All of you, listen!"

Looking up, Gar saw it was one of their scouts, stationed well outside of camp to see anything that happened in the wood around them. With the rest of the rankers and recruits, he snapped straight, standing still, but the sergeants and officers only came walking over, alert and wary.

"General Malachi's coming!" the sentry called. "Police the camp! Polish your leather and brass!"

The captain exchanged a glance with his lieutenant.

"Not that much to police," the younger man said. "We've been keeping things in shape."

"I hope your sergeants have been inspecting their men's gear," the captain said. "Get them busy!"

There followed a hectic hour while everything that had been overlooked was swept and scoured and everything clean was cleaned again. Gar hauled water and scrubbed where he was told like a beast of burden, wondering if it was time to disappear again—but he remembered the ashes of the youth village and his anger began to burn again. He had burst away from the bandit general's men before and he could do it again if he had to. Meanwhile, what could he say to bamboozle the man into keeping him near?

Then General Malachi rode into the camp surrounded by his bodyguards. The first soldier to see him shouted, "General!" and everyone ran to their places in line.

They snapped to attention as the general dismounted and swaggered along their rows, enjoying the panic he'd created. He looked up and down soldier after soldier, snapping out a criticism here, a nitpick there—leather not polished mirror bright, spear edge not honed to razor sharpness. Gar watched him come, surprised that the general hadn't picked him out already, tense for a fight but sure of what he was going to say, the proof he could offer that he wasn't a danger. Crel was next; after him, General Malachi would be looking up into Gar's face. . . .

Crel stood at attention, spear slanted outward. Malachi stopped in front of him, holding his hands open for the spear. "Present arms!"

"Sir!" Crel said, and presented the weapon point-first, straight into Malachi's ribs.

Malachi's scream broke into a gurgle even as his bodyguard shouted and fell upon Crel. The young man went down under a wave of men while the captains ran to cradle the general in their arms, arguing furiously about whether or not to pull out the spear. They closed around him, hiding him from view, and Gar stood paralyzed, hearing the thoughts of a dying man and his last guttural words: *Kill him!*

Then the captains stood, moving away from the corpse, and Major Ivack came over to the soldiers who had yanked Crel to his feet. The youth was bruised and bleeding but still alive enough to spit in Ivack's face.

The major backhanded him casually, then caught his hair and yanked his head back, demanding, "Why?"

"Because you burned my village and slew my friends," Crel gasped.

Ivack digested that, holding the youth's head still, then snarled, "Who put you up to it?"

"The Scarlet Company!" Crel shouted.

Furious, Ivack backhanded him again, then said to his captors, "Torture him until he tells their names."

"Quince the Potter in Cellin Village," Crel said through swollen lips. "Ivor the Cooper of Cellin. Joco Smith of Cellin."

"You won't escape the torture that way," Ivack snarled, then called out to all his men, "What kind of loyalty is this? He names his cohorts in an instant just to save himself a little pain!"

None of the soldiers answered, none breathed even a word. All knew that the pain would not be little and knew the legend even better—that the Scarlet Company's people always gave names readily.

Ivack swung back to Crel. "You'll die in agony for this, laddie."

"Stopping Malachi is worth my life," Crel retorted.

Ivack backhanded him across the mouth yet again. "We'll see

if you still say that when we've used you for a threshing floor." He turned to Crel's captors. "Throw him down and beat him with flails."

Doom-faced, the soldiers hustled Crel away.

Ivack turned to a captain. "Send twenty riders to Cellin and bring those men."

The captain turned away to shout orders. The rankers stood frozen, faces expressionless, all with sinking spirits. They knew that the riders would find the potter, the cooper, and the smith fled, all gone on sudden errands. In fact, given the reputation of Malachi and his band, they might find the whole village deserted. They might burn it for revenge, but no one would die.

Except Crel.

Major Ivack came back from the interrogation in the middle of the day, his face thunderous. The soldiers gravitated to the men who had given the beatings, who were swilling ale after their hot work and more than willing to talk about the horror they had visited.

"We beat him to pudding," said the one Gar found, a stocky bandit named Gorbo. "He told us his name right off—Crel, it is—but we beat him for it. Then Ivack asked him what else he knew about the Scarlet Company. He told us that the cooper, the potter, and the smith had all taught him ways to kill with one blow, but that he'd only needed the smith's way—one short stab with every ounce of his strength behind it. Major told us to beat him after the answer, since we hadn't needed to beat him before it."

"Who gave the orders to the potter, the cooper, and the smith?" someone asked.

"That we could beat him for," Gorbo said, "because he didn't know."

"They never do," another soldier muttered.

"He told us he had joined the Scarlet Company only for the privilege of killing the general," Gorbo went on. "That's what he called it—a privilege—and he didn't know nor care who'd guv the three their orders. We gave him a privilege of another half-dozen blows, we did."

"Who told him how to get in among us?" a soldier asked.

"The cooper, he said," Gorbo answered. "The cooper told Crel that the Scarlet Company had known some young man would come along with a lot of hatred and nothing to lose, that he would be the one to slay the bandit chief. We beat him another dozen blows for that one, too." He took a swig of ale, stared off into the distance, then delivered his judgment of the ordeal: "That didn't make him know nothing more about the Scarlet Company, though."

"There anything left of him?" Gar asked, already planning a rescue.

"There's some life," Gorbo allowed, "and we didn't break his legs. Major Ivack wants to hang him fancy. Something about drawing him and quartering. Don't know how he means to do that."

"We'll find out tomorrow," another soldier said.

Gorbo shook his head. "Before sunset. The major wants to chop him while General Malachi's ghost is still around to see."

The men shuddered, looking around them, and making signs against evil.

Then you had no time to save him, Alea thought, her heart breaking.

I didn't need to, Gar said, and let her remember the rest with him.

Major Ivack had taken command. He didn't seem to be aware of any increase in status, didn't puff himself up or strut, only strode angrily about the camp looking for objects on which to vent his wrath, giving orders in short, clipped phrases. Nonetheless, Gar had the feeling he was about to promote himself to general.

The most pronounced order had been to throw a rope over a tree limb and lay a workbench before it. Gar wondered where the man had heard about drawing and quartering but realized that this was the sort of gruesome tale that passed down from generation to generation without any planning—and resisted efforts to weed it out. Major Ivack looked like the sort who would have listened to such tales with avid attention.

Gar didn't like him.

He liked him even less when Ivack took up station before the table, surrounded by the bodyguards who had been General Malachi's. The sergeants bawled orders and marched their men into place around the ancient oak with the noose hanging from its limb. The soldiers stood at ease, glowering and somber, as Gorbo and another ranker frog-marched Crel out of a tent, face dark and swollen with bruises. Up to the oak they hauled him, hands tied behind his back, and stood him with his back to the trunk, facing Ivack. They set the noose about his neck, then snugged it up.

"Do you have any last words?" Ivack snarled.

Crel managed to cough the words out of a swollen mouth. "Death to the brutes who kill the innocent!"

"Hoist him up!" Ivack roared, and the bodyguard nearest him pivoted, jamming his dagger into the major's heart.

17

The whole company was silent, shocked at the suddenness of it, and they all heard the bodyguard say, very clearly, "Malachi was too careful. You weren't."

A captain found words. "Wh—why?"

"He led the troops who conquered my village." The bodyguard lifted his head, glaring around. "All right, they'd cast me out, but they were *mine,* damn it! That's when I joined the Scarlet Company."

"Grab him!" the captain roared.

The bodyguard brought his spear to guard. "You really want to?" He turned to the captain. "Come and take me! But remember—I may not be the only one here from the Scarlet Company. I was waiting my moment—who else?"

The whole company stood, wavering, irresolute. Gar could feel fear balancing outrage, saw each bandit glancing at the men to left and right of him, saw the twitch of the head as each tried to look behind without others seeing—and felt the moment when fear won out and men eased back just a little.

The bodyguard felt it, too. He turned, stalking over to Crel and drawing his dagger. Crel braced himself, but the bodyguard jabbed his spear in the ground, took hold of the rope, and sawed through it with half a dozen quick strokes. Crel tottered and almost fell against him.

The bodyguard hoisted him over a shoulder and took up his spear again. He glared around him and said, "We're going now. If you try to follow, be careful who walks beside you." Then he turned and strode away into the woods.

There was a collective intake of breath, of leaning forward, of waiting for an order—but every man glanced at those beside him again, then turned to the captain.

The captain glared darkly after the two men of the Scarlet Company but said nothing. After a little while, he turned and stalked back to his tent.

The men relaxed, began to talk to one another in hushed tones, to mill about. Gar gazed about him, seeming blank and confused, but listening intently for any mention of the Scarlet Company, anyone thinking it was his duty to draw a dagger.

He heard no one. The bluff had worked.

Of course, the bodyguard hadn't known it was a bluff.

Alea absorbed it all, dazed. Finally she thought, *Gar, what are we doing here?*

I've been wondering that myself, Gar answered. *I'll meet you tonight and we can talk it over face to face.*

Meet me? How? You're a soldier!

Men are beginning to leave already, Gar told her, *just packing up their gear and walking off into the forest. Nobody seems to care about stopping them.*

Without General Malachi, the whole army is falling apart, Alea thought, still numb.

Certainly after Ivack tried to hold it together. No one wants to be the third-time charm. I can certainly walk away after dark. Where shall we rendezvous?

I'm at the Inn of the North Star, Alea told him. *Let me know when you get here and I'll come out to meet you in the common room.*

She had a few hours before he came, though. Dazed, Alea made her way down to the river, then followed it upstream, stopping frequently to stare at the water as though it could reveal the mysteries of human greed and cruelty—or at least swallow them and let them dissolve. Then she walked again, letting the sound of the running water lull her, soothe her spirit. When the brook ran in among the trees, she accepted the shade and the murmuring of the leaves as balm. She knelt on a rock and dipped a hand in the stream, letting it run through her fingers. At last she stood up with a sigh—and saw Evanescent.

"You meant it, didn't you?" With no one nearby to hear, she could speak her thoughts aloud. "That you *are* the Scarlet Company."

Us, and all of you, Evanescent replied, even you newly come, for it seems you have joined them now.

"Why not?" Alea demanded, somewhat irked. "They're the only ones doing anything to cleanse this planet of the evil ones!"

So say many, but not until they have encountered that evil themselves, Evanescent replied. We remind them, that is all—remind them of evil, and of their dedication to their fellows.

Alea frowned. "You mean you're the ones who keep the men and women of the Scarlet Company from trying to use it as a tool to gain power and riches for themselves?"

When there are no evil and greedy men prowling the land, Evanescent explained, people can grow complacent and forget their zeal for others' freedom, forget there is something greater than themselves, greater than any one human being or even any one family. An encounter with a strange and powerful being reminds them and renews their devotion.

"You scare them back into line," Alea interpreted.

Or overawe them and make them rededicate themselves, Evanescent said, for surely if beings of such power as our kind can forgo glory and dominion in search of a greater good, smaller and weaker beings such as people can do so, too.

"You put the fear of the gods in them."

The awe, perhaps. Fear is the smallest part of that. Then they forget us, but the zeal remains.

"Neatly done," Alea said with a cynical smile, "to forget you but remember your impact. What do you gain from it, though?"

A reason for living, mortal woman, the alien native replied, for we may be of different kinds and birthed by different worlds, but we are both living souls, and the welfare of one is the welfare of All—and that All overawes even we of fur and teeth, for we are also of mind and soul.

"And therefore dedicated to the goodness of all," Alea said thoughtfully. "What do you do with those who seek to exploit and hurt their fellows, though?"

Why should we do anything? Evanescent returned. You have seen, through your mate's eyes. The human folk will sooner or later go to the Scarlet Company, who shall train them to turn on the tyrants.

"But they can't always be successful," Alea objected. "Even Malachi stopped the first three assassins. And I somehow doubt that only one man in a hundred years will try to gain power."

There are many, Evanescent admitted, but most are careless and wander in the forest alone.

Alea shuddered.

Even them we do not eat, Evanescent told her, the tone a rebuke. We bury them deeply, after the fashion of your kind—and their deaths are quick and sudden; many do not even know they have died.

"But the careful ones," Alea inferred, "they become like General Malachi."

Always they raise up enough hatred so that some think it worth their lives to kill them,

"Yes," Alea said, "but more in the town. When I visited the sick with the priestess this afternoon, a dying man recruited me into the Scarlet Company to fill his place."

Gar stared. Alea especially enjoyed the way his mouth opened and closed without any words. Finally he managed to ask, "Why? What did he know about you?"

"He was one of the people I talked to when I was trying to raise the alarm," Alea explained. "He told his cell about me, and they told the other cells—and he found out nearly every step I took. He knew I'd become a priestess and was visiting the sick. He decided I had the good of the people at heart and sent me to a friend of his to be inducted properly into the Company."

"What . . . sort of inductance?" Gar asked, his voice strangled.

"Lecture and discussion—mostly lecture, actually. The Scarlet Company's history and structure, how to meet the rest of my cell, how to call for help if I need it or if someone else does—everything to make me function within the organization."

"It *is* organized, then?"

"Very much so—but it's decentralized," Alea explained. "They've divided the land into nineteen districts, each taking care only of itself and keeping down any bullies who try to take over. The local chapter was on the verge of calling in a couple of other districts to help them when one of their agents went with us to the ruins of the youths' village and found Crel. She recruited him into the Scarlet Company, and you know the rest."

"So it wouldn't be terribly easy for any one person to take over the Scarlet Company and use it as an instrument of conquest," Gar said slowly, "not if he could only give orders within his own district."

Alea nodded. "If any agent tried to gain power, another province, or several, would unite to bring him down."

"One of their own?" Gar asked skeptically.

"Especially one of their own," Alea confirmed. "They're sworn to serve the public and chastise bullies, after all, and any one of them who tried to become a tyrant would be a traitor."

"That would help," Gar said slowly, "but I could think of ways around it."

"No one else has," Alea said, "they think."

"Think?" Gar asked with raised eyebrows.

"Twice, some agent has come up with a scheme to unite all the districts under one supreme cell," Alea told him. "Their cell-mates stopped talking to them, and so did everyone else in the Scarlet Company."

"Ostracized," Gar said, impressed. "Cut off, cut out."

"But not killed," Alea reminded him. "One of them retaliated by organizing the bandits the way General Malachi did and conquered a village. *Then* they killed him."

"No difficulty finding a volunteer that time?"

"None."

"Still no guarantee." Gar looked out over the town.

"It seems to work," Alea retorted. "It has, for centuries."

"Yes, it has." Gar turned back to her and she saw that he was grinning.

"You're happy about this!" she accused.

"Delighted," Gar assured her. "I have been put to the test of my convictions."

"Yes." Alea nodded. "You've found a people whose political system suits them."

"Their lack of a political system, rather," Gar said, "but it does protect their civil rights, as long as they're content with Neolithic village culture."

"Which they are, as long as they have advanced medicine and farming methods," Alea said. "I'll admit that this couldn't work even in Midgard, where they need to be able to call all the able-bodied men to war on a day's notice—but this system avoids war."

"It could never work for a modern society of metropolises, industry, and international commerce, of course," Gar said. "That calls for large-scale organization and complicated ways of coordinating people—what we usually think of as government."

"The Scarlet Company would be killing a would-be tyrant every day," Alea agreed, "and the government would very quickly learn how to hunt down the Company members and jail them, then execute them."

"But these people's ancestors made sure they wouldn't develop that way," Gar said, "and it suits them—as long as they're content to live in villages and small towns and never travel much except for a year or two in their youth."

Alea nodded, looking out over the town, where lights were beginning to go out. "It stays in balance. It works." She turned to Gar, unable to resist needling him. "Of course, the individual villages and towns are functioning democracies."

"Very *primitive* democracies," Gar protested, "and I had nothing to do with setting them up. Besides, my guiding principle has always been to make sure the government suits the people and the society, and this one definitely does."

"That principle is being put to the test," Alea said with wicked glee. "How are you rating? Will you pass?"

"I shall leave this planet tonight," Gar averred, "without trying to make any changes." He pulled up the tab of his shirt collar and spoke into it. "Come and get us, Herkimer, would you?"

"Descending," the collar answered in a thin and tinny voice.

Alea looked upward, waiting for the spaceship to come into view. "Their form of democracy does suit them, Gar."

Gar nodded. "Especially since the assassins have become the government."

Alea turned to him in shock. "They have not! The Scarlet Company is sworn to prevent government!"

"And thereby protects the people from the worst of the bandits," Gar pointed out, "and from powermongers in the villages—and in the process, they resolve disputes that go beyond the village councils' power and would turn into blood feuds if no one intervened."

"The sages do that!"

"But the Scarlet Company calls them in," Gar reminded her. "Admittedly, it's a minimal form of government, but it's more complex than it seems, requiring teamwork between the priests, the priestesses, the sages, the village councils—but the center is the Scarlet Company. In fact, I find it hard to believe a balance like that can work without open coordination—but it does." He shrugged. "I certainly have no business trying to tell them that it doesn't."

They stood side by side, watching the stars as something began to blot them out in an ever-widening circle. Then it wasn't a blot of darkness anymore, but a spaceship descending with its lights out.

Alea watched it fall, feeling a little angry again that Gar had salved his feelings by pretending that a secret society of assassins could be a government. She was tempted to tell him, out of sheer spite, what she had learned in those last few minutes they had been at the inn, when she had overheard the thoughts of the innkeeper's wife, one of her serving maids, and four other village women. They had locked the door of an inner room and, as they stitched and knitted, discussed the afternoon's assassination and whether or not the Scarlet Company had stayed true to its ideals.

She had kept track of the discussion as she had climbed the hillside beside Gar in silence, and had eavesdropped as they decided that the Company had indeed remained pure, so that no intervention would be needed.

She decided she wouldn't tell him—he would just pretend that it was only one more part of his informal government, anyway. It would have been satisfying to see the look on his face until he managed to think of that—but she felt petty even considering the idea. Besides, Gar didn't really need to know that the founders had set up a second secret society to keep watch on the first—that the Scarlet Company might be watching over the people, but that the Indigo Company was watching the Scarlet.